The Curse at White Pines

KINDRED SPIRITS MYSTERIES

BETH CONNOR

WOLF GROVE MEDIA, LLC

Contents

CHAPTER ONE

New Beginnings

Sienna Avery approached White Pine Resort and crossed into a realm where reality seemed to soften. As her green Toyota shuddered down the winding driveway, she clutched the steering wheel and muttered under her breath. "Just a bit further, don't quit on me now."

The morning sun bathed the resort's facade in a warm glow, unveiling its timeless architecture. Lush forests embraced the grounds, and she felt the trails calling out to her, inviting her to explore the wilderness beyond. There would be time for hikes, but for now, she would focus on the task at hand. Income.

Sienna's college was a mere 45-minute drive from White Pines. This job not only offered her the convenience of a place to live while campus was closed, but a much-needed escape. The winding mountain roads were her sanctuary. Every curve brought a sense of peace and each turn helped the pressures of paying for school melt away. It was summer break, and she relished the freedom to embark on an adventure. When she had steered through the scenic route, there was a thrill of discovery with each mile.

She wanted—no, needed—control. The open road, the guarantee that if things became too overwhelming or if she needed a respite, she could escape into the embrace of the nearby woods. The idea of relying on others for transportation, of being trapped or limited in her movements, dampened her spirit.

As she parked and stepped out, a sudden chill ran down her spine, unexpected given the summer warmth. The trees seemed to whisper secrets, and for a fleeting moment, she felt as if someone—or something—was watching her long before she arrived.

Her eyes darted around, seeking the source of her unease. There was an undercurrent of something... otherworldly?

As Sienna approached the entrance, her bag held close to her chest. She sensed the beginnings of an extraordinary summer. Romance and adventure beckoned, and as shadows danced across the walls of White Pine Resorts, she realized that the stories here were more than just tales—they were alive.

White Pine Resort was full of history and old stories. Whispers of legends, some lost and others just beginning. Star-crossed lovers, brave soldiers, and free spirits—all had found their lives interwoven within the walls and woods of the resort. Every brick, every leaf, every gust of wind carried that energy. The love that transcended time, and promises made beneath the same sky.

As the sun continued its ascent, the grounds came alive. Birds, perhaps the true custodians of its secrets, sang melodies old and new, their songs harmonizing with the rustle of leaves and the gentle gurgle of streams. Deer grazed upon dew-kissed meadows.

The resort seemed to grow from the land. Ivy draped the walls, flowers burst forth in vivid colors, and ancient trees stood sentinel, their boughs stretching over the heart of the resort. For those fortunate enough to witness the dawn at White Pine Resorts, the experience was nothing short of enchanting. It was a reminder that amidst luxury, the true magic lay in nature's embrace.

Sienna left the parking lot in awe of the lavishness that unfurled before her. Even at this hour, the place seemed to buzz with energy. She was struck by confusion and had expected clear signs to guide the summer help, but if there were any, she had missed them. Most of the newcomers arrived by shuttle, which probably had its own designated entrance and directions. With a soft sigh, she trusted her instincts and followed a path that looked more well-trodden than the others.

She passed a manicured garden, and observed gardeners at work, their hands moving with practiced ease as they pruned roses and arranged blooms. Their dedication was clear. Sienna could almost smell the fragrance of the earth and blossoms.

The sound of cleaning drew her attention next. Housekeepers were busy ensuring that every window gleamed, and every hallway echoed the resort's standard of perfection. Their meticulousness spoke volumes, and they moved with grace, their work a dance of precision.

Lost in her observations, she didn't realize she had wandered into a more private part of the resort until a voice startled her. "Miss! This area is off-limits." She turned to see a security guard gesturing her away from a set of double doors. Emblazoned on the entrance was the unmistakable crest of the Whitmores. The opulence visible through the doors was unlike anything Sienna had ever seen—ornate chandeliers, grand portraits, and a glimpse of what looked like a golden staircase.

Flushing with embarrassment, Sienna mumbled an apology. As she hurried away, her thoughts were a mix of awe and disdain. The Whitmores weren't just the owners; they were monarchs of their domain. Their wealth wasn't just from White Pine Resorts, but from an empire of luxury and old money. While the world around her sang of nature and hard work, the Whitmores' wing sang of excess and entitlement.

Sienna's heart rate steadied as she took in the sprawling expanse of the resort. She needed directions, and she needed them now. An elderly man that was tending to a patch of foxgloves nearby drew her attention. He had a wise, weathered face and an ease in his movements that suggested he'd known this place for years, maybe decades.

"Excuse me," Sienna began, "could you point me towards where the summer help shuttle arrives?"

The old man looked up, his eyes bright beneath bushy gray eyebrows. "Ah, Lot B, eh? Just follow this path," he pointed with a gnarled finger, "and turn left when you see the large oak. Can't miss it."

"Thank you," she murmured.

With renewed purpose, she made her way down the path. The sounds of laughter and excited chatter grew louder as she neared the designated spot. As she rounded the bend, she arrived just in time to see a large shuttle bus emblazoned with the White Pine Resorts logo pulling in. The door hissed open, and out stepped a wave of fresh-faced young people, a mix of excitement and nervous anticipation painted on their features.

Sienna stood a little apart from the arriving crowd. Her long, chestnut hair cascaded in soft waves down her back, catching the early sunlight and creating a warm halo around her. As she watched the new arrivals, a flutter of emotions danced within her. She felt a kinship with these newcomers, yet she felt a world apart, having driven herself here and already experienced a taste of White Pines Resort—its beauty and its opulence, its history and its present.

A sharp, professional voice interrupted her thoughts. "Good morning, everyone! I trust you all had a pleasant journey." The voice belonged to a tall, well-dressed woman with graying hair pulled into a bun. Her name tag read 'Clarice - HR Manager.'

She approached Sienna first, extending a manicured hand. "You must be Sienna Avery. They informed me you'd be coming in your own vehicle." Sienna nodded, taking the woman's hand and feeling the firm grip. "Yes, that's me."

"Very well. Let's not waste time. We have a lot to cover," Clarice announced, addressing the gathering. Her efficiency was clear, and Sienna sensed that beneath the veneer of professionalism, Clarice might have a warmer side.

Clarice ushered them through a grand set of double doors, revealing interiors as breathtaking as the exterior. Crystal chandeliers hung above, casting rainbows across the polished marble floors. Majestic fireplaces anchored the grand rooms, each adorned with paintings of the White Mountains.

As they explored, Sienna found herself drawn to the colors and textures of the sofas and drapes, her fingers tracing the plush fabrics. The meticulous attention to detail was everywhere, from the intricate woodwork to the ceiling frescoes. Each room seemed to have its own story, pulling Sienna deeper into the allure of White Pine.

Art the end of the tour, Clarice led them to a wing dedicated to the staff. "Here," she announced, "is where you'll collect your uniforms. Wear them with pride. These represent your identity as employees here at White Pine Resort."

Sienna picked up a folded set—crisp white shirts, tailored skirts for the ladies, trousers for the men, and a deep green velvet vest reflecting the hue of the surrounding pines. As they continued the orientation, Sienna's mind wandered—between the history in the hallways, the grandeur of her surroundings, and the adventure that awaited.

Her first few hours on the job were a flurry of activity. White Pine Resort was always buzzing with guests from various parts of the world, each with their unique set of expectations.

Amanda, a slender woman with a sparkle in her eyes, was Sienna's assigned mentor. Boasting five years of experience, Amanda was a wellspring of wisdom and practical advice. Flashing a smile, she shared her first rule: "Always wear comfortable shoes. We do a lot of walking and standing."

Sienna learned what Amanda had hinted at earlier. Their shifts were exhausting, packed with endless interactions, coordinating activities, and ensuring each guest felt valued. Sienna's first error occurred when she booked the same suite for two different families. The situation was tense, with both families upset. However, thanks to Amanda's diplomacy and seasoned approach, they upgraded one family to a superior suite and calmed the other with complimentary perks.

Throughout these trials, Sienna absorbed valuable lessons. The most crucial? People weren't just in pursuit of luxury—they craved meaningful experiences, memories, and connections.

Her shift concluded with a challenging encounter with a demanding guest. Once resolved, Sienna sought refuge on a secluded balcony of the resort. It offered a breathtaking view over expansive pines. A short while later, Amanda joined her, her eyes reflecting understanding.

"Sienna," Amanda started, her voice gentle yet seasoned, "this job is about more than just fulfilling requests or managing bookings. You're stepping into our guests' stories. Each one arrives here with their own personalities, some soft and some bold. If you really listen, you'll understand them. The better you understand, the better you can serve."

Sienna gazed out at the forest, its whispers of ancient tales floating through the air, older than any guest that had ever checked in. As she looked, her dream of becoming a travel writer stirred within her. She envisioned days filled not with serving at resorts like this one, but with reveling in them, capturing her adventures on paper, and inviting the world to share in the enchantment she felt now.

"See you tomorrow, Sienna," Amanda whispered, squeezing her shoulder before departing.

Left alone, the calm of the night enveloped Sienna. The play of the pool's reflection in the soft moonlight suggested that the stars had come down for a swim. The mountains, ever-present, stood guard, their peaks veiled in a dreamy mist.

A sudden drop in temperature made her shiver. Alongside the coolness, an aroma wafted around—a peculiar blend of lavender and old parchment. It was both comforting and eerie. A fleeting shadow, almost too quick to be real, passed by the corner of her vision.

She brushed it off as her tired mind playing tricks, but then another soft sound startled her. Pivoting, her gaze met that of a man she hadn't seen earlier. With his dark hair and deep blue eyes, he appeared to blend into the resort's atmosphere of mystery and charm.

He offered her a nod and their shared connection was a brief but intense, a wordless communication in the twilight quiet. Sienna felt an uncanny sense of familiarity, like an echo from a dream she couldn't quite remember.

With a tilt of his head and a small smile, he turned and left, leaving Sienna with a swirl of questions. She tried to follow his path with her eyes and noted he walked towards a corridor lined with portraits. One painting, in particular, drew her attention—a figure from a past era with a strong resemblance to the stranger.

A whisper of wind brought with it soft murmurs. Sienna shook her head, laughing at her own fanciful thoughts. Yet, the magnetic pull of the man remained, leaving her with the promise that this summer at White Pine would unveil more mysteries than she'd expected. *Time to snap back to reality*, she mused, pushing open the doors to the bustling heart of the resort's employee wing.

The noise of the staff cafeteria was a contrast to the expansive silence of the resort's balconies and hallways. Sienna, tray in hand, hesitated, scanning the room for a familiar face. Just as she was contemplating sitting alone, a cheerful voice broke her reverie.

"Hey! You're the new one, right? Over here!" A girl waved her over, her name tag shining: *Maya*.

Sienna made her way over. "Hi, yes, I'm Sienna. First day."

"You survived then? Good start!" Maya grinned. "How'd it go?"

They laughed, and as Sienna relaxed. "Actually..." she started, "I had this encounter on one of the balconies. A man, tall and very good looking. I'm worried he might be a guest. We're not supposed to—"

"Fraternize with the guests," Maya finished for her, nodding. "I know, they drum that rule for us from day one. Can you describe him?"

Her words painted an image of the stranger, and Maya looked thoughtful for a moment. "Doesn't ring a bell. But if you're that curious, the summer staff kick-off party is tomorrow night. It's the perfect chance to spot him, especially if he's part of the staff."

Sienna's heart fluttered at the possibility. "I just want to make sure I didn't break any rules on my first day," she said. A tiny part of her hoped to see him again.

Maya patted her hand. "Don't sweat it too much. Just enjoy your time here. And who knows? Maybe tomorrow's party will clear things up for you."

Boosted by her new friendship with Maya, Sienna left the cafeteria, feeling excited about the upcoming event. She traversed the resort's hallways, the echo of her footsteps on the marble floors amplified in the quiet. The grandeur took on an almost mystical quality, its windows shimmering like a constellation of stars brought down to earth.

With a sigh, she opened the door to her shared quarters, appreciating the thoughtful layout that offered each occupant some privacy. She moved toward her assigned area, where gauzy drapes around her bed created a private sanctuary within the room.

Sienna sank into her soft mattress, her mind buzzing as it replayed the day's happenings. The resort, the lively conversations in the staff cafeteria, and Amanda's wise counsel all mingled in her thoughts. But it was the fleeting encounter with the stranger that captivated her the most.

That brief connection had sparked something inside her, stirring a flurry of emotions. Who was he? She wondered.

Boosted by Maya's friendship, Sienna left the cafeteria, feeling excited about the upcoming event.

As Sienna traversed the resort's hallways, the echo of her footsteps on the marble floors seemed amplified in the quiet. The grandeur of White Pine Resorts took on a mystical quality, its windows shimmering like a constellation of stars brought down to earth.

With a sigh, she opened the door to her shared quarters, appreciating the thoughtful layout that offered each occupant some privacy. She moved toward her assigned area, where gauzy drapes around her bed created a private sanctuary within the room.

Sienna sank into her soft mattress, her mind buzzing as it replayed the day's happenings. The elegant architecture of the resort, the lively conversations in the staff cafeteria, and Amanda's wise counsel all mingled in her thoughts. But it was the fleeting encounter with the stranger that captivated her the most. That brief connection had sparked something inside her, stirring a flurry of emotions. Who was he? She wondered, sensing that he was another piece in the intriguing puzzle that was White Pine Resorts.

The day's exertions weighed on her as she pulled the soft duvet around her and coaxed her eyelids to close. Yet, as she hovered on the edge of sleep, her heart fluttered with excitement for the days ahead. This summer promised a journey of discovery, adventure, and possibly, a romance. With these thoughts, Sienna drifted into a deep, dream-laden sleep.

CHAPTER TWO

A Party Under the Stars

T he morning had been a gentler introduction than yesterday for Sienna. With most White Pine Resort closed for summer employee training day, the usual bustle of guests and activities was subdued. The owners dedicated most areas of the property to orientation sessions, training seminars, and team-building exercises. Only a select few areas remained open to cater to the minimal number of guests checked in; the seasoned, year-round employees managed these areas.

As a part of this training day, new and returning employees familiarized themselves with the vast property, not just in terms of their specific roles, but also to connect with the very essence of what made White Pine so special.

One highlight of the orientation was discovering a hike locals called Frozen Tears. It was part of the Appalachian Trail—which she hoped to conquer in its entirety some-day. This trail was also steeped in lore, rumored to be haunted by the ghost of a jilted lover. Such tales of haunt-ings and tragic love merged her twin passions for the para-normal and hiking. She was determined to explore the trail herself.

Despite the reduced guest count, the resort radiated an air of excitement. The annual Employee Kick-Off Party was just hours away. To make sure every staff member, from managers to gardeners, could take part in the festivi-ties, the Whitmores had hired outside caterers and tempo-rary staff. This evening, hierarchies would blur, allowing every employee a taste of the luxury White Pine's guests reveled in daily.

A smirk played on her lips as Sienna processed the de-tails of the evening's grand event. *Ah, the benevolence of the uber-rich,* she mused. *Giving us common folk a taste of their world for one magical night.* It felt like a theatrical performance that the Whitmores would elevate their staff to guest status, a charitable gesture to appease the masses. But for all her inner cynicism, Sienna couldn't suppress the flutter of excitement in her stomach. After all, who wouldn't be intrigued by a night of mingling in luxury, even if it was just a taste? The allure was undeniable, and Sienna couldn't wait for the festivities to begin.

As the sun began its descent, Sienna was ready for the night. The resort transformed under the waning light. Lanterns glowed, casting dancing shadows on the pathways. Distant sounds of a guitar tuning provided a soft backdrop to the murmur of eager conversations.

The guests of honor tonight, the employees themselves, emerged in their finest attire. Elegant dresses, sharp suits, and radiant smiles were the order of the evening. Sienna watched as tables laden with gourmet delights were set up, each dish looking more tantalizing than the last.

A little away, the promise of music and dance awaited under a canopy adorned with twinkling fairy lights. It beckoned everyone to forget their roles for a night and just lose themselves in the evening.

The Whitmores had orchestrated a night where barriers were forgotten. As Sienna looked around, taking it all in, she felt a deep sense of gratitude. She had a cushy, competitive summer job, a place to lay her head, and a fantastic party to attend. Summer was yet to kick into full gear, but tonight, Sienna felt right at home.

The cool evening air brushed against Sienna as she made her way to the heart of the party. Her outfit reflected her unique sense of style. She had chosen a flowy, knee-length dress in a subtle shade of olive, its simple cut enhanced by delicate embroidery at the neckline and hem. Strappy flat sandals and her signature messy bun completed the look. A pendant, gifted from her grandmother, hung against her collarbone, catching the soft light now and then.

Sienna's polished look was just the surface. Underneath, she was a mix of emotions: excitement for the evening, a touch of nervous energy, and a deep, persistent curiosity. She scanned the crowd more often than she'd like, searching for a particular face, unable to forget those piercing blue eyes and that captivating presence.

Making her way through the crowd of elegantly dressed guests, she spotted a familiar face. It was Maya who had quickly become a friend, their connection sparked by a shared sense of humor. Maya waved her over, beaming.

"Sienna!" Maya called out. "You clean up well! Who are you trying to impress?"

Sienna laughed, feeling a blush creep up her cheeks. "Oh, hush! I could say the same about you." She winked, taking in Maya's stunning crimson dress.

The two shared a light-hearted moment, trading observations about the evening and the surrounding extravagance. As they sipped on their drinks, they exchanged playful bets on which dish on the banquet table would be the first to run out, and chuckled at some of the more flamboyant dance moves on display.

Yet, even as Sienna reveled in the comfort of Maya's company, a part of her remained alert, her eyes drifting across the crowd. The mysterious stranger had left a mark on her mind, and the night was still young. She was mid-conversation with Maya when the atmosphere shifted. A tall figure, well dressed, stepped into the spotlight of the party.

Sienna's heart skipped a beat, recognizing those eyes that she had locked onto earlier that day. The memory of their fleeting encounter, so vivid, made her stomach flutter with excitement. Unable to contain herself, she nudged Maya, pointing in his direction. "That's him! That's the guy I was telling you about."

Maya's eyes widened, her playful demeanor overshadowed by a more dramatic tone. "Oh... oh no. That's Dylan. Dylan... Whitmore." Her voice rose with each repetition of his name.

Sienna blinked, a bit taken aback. "Dylan Whitmore? As in, the Whitmores who own this place?" An involuntary wrinkle of distaste formed on her forehead. She had never been fond of the ultra-rich, finding their lifestyles excessive and often out of touch with reality.

Maya leaned closer, her voice thick with warning. "That very one. And honey, let me tell you, that man is trouble with a capital T. He's got the looks, the wealth, and the charm to draw anyone in. But he leaves a trail of broken hearts wherever he goes."

Sienna's lips pressed into a thin line. "Great. Just what I need. Thanks for the heads up, Maya."

Maya patted her hand. "Just watch your back around him. And maybe your heart, too." She winked, but her playful smile didn't quite reach her eyes.

Sienna mulled over Maya's words, a knot of disappointment forming in her stomach. Yet, despite the warning, every time her eyes settled on Dylan, her chest thrummed with an undeniable excitement. Damn it! She observed him weaving through the crowd, his magnetic aura undeniable. Every so often, his gaze would scan the room, seeming to search for something—or perhaps someone.

As the evening progressed, Sienna couldn't help but steal glances in Dylan's direction. And each time their eyes met, a silent spark passed between them. The warning echoed in her mind, but his allure was undeniable.

The music quickened, and Sienna caught the attention of a handsome man with chiseled features and sun-bronzed skin. His hazel eyes sparkled, and his wavy, sandy-blonde hair looked as though he'd just come from a day at the beach. "Care to dance?" he asked, grinning as he extended his hand.

Taken aback, Sienna's thoughts lingered on Dylan, but she welcomed the diversion. "I'd love to," she replied, smiling as she placed her hand in his.

The stranger introduced himself as Ben, a new lifeguard at the resort. As they danced, his athletic grace and easy way struck Sienna as he led her across the dance floor. He had a playful and light-hearted energy that was infectious. She laughed at his jokes and admired how his shirt hugged his toned torso.

Ben was her type: sporty, charming, and attractive. She tried to immerse herself in the moment, but her mind wandered.

As they spun around the dance floor, Sienna's gaze drifted back to Dylan. She wasn't alone. Many eyes seemed to be fixed on him, but one woman held his attention. She was stunning, with long, raven-black hair and red lips. She wore a figure-hugging dress that left little to the imagination. The two danced, their bodies merging. Sienna watched as the woman tilted her head back, allowing Dylan access to her neck, and his hand rested on the small of her back, pulling her even closer. Their dance was more than just intimate—it was a sultry grind.

A pang of something inexplicable — jealousy or longing, perhaps — surged through Sienna. She tried to focus on Ben, but the way she felt toward Dylan was undeniable.

Ben, sensing her distraction, leaned in. "You okay?"

She nodded and gave him a reassuring smile. "Yeah, just lost in thought. Let's keep dancing."

As the night wore on and the music transitioned into a slow, haunting melody, Sienna felt a shift in the atmosphere. She was drawn toward the bar area where Dylan was now standing. His previous dance partner was nowhere in sight.

Their eyes met across the room, recognition and intrigue clear. The world around Sienna blurred, the noise and the chatter fading into the background.

As they came face to face, Sienna's vivacity took charge. "Hey," she greeted him, "Seems like we keep running into each other."

Dylan's lips curved into a smile. "It would appear so," he replied, his voice deep and smooth. He took a moment to look her up and down. "You look incredible."

Sienna felt a blush creep up her neck. "Thank you," she responded. "Not so bad yourself, Mr. Whitmore."

The moment the words "Mr. Whitmore" slipped from Sienna's lips. Dylan's expression shifted. A slight downturn of his mouth and a flash of vulnerability she hadn't seen before overshadowed the playfulness in his eyes. It was as though a curtain had been drawn back, revealing a more complex character behind those confident blue eyes.

Sienna picked up on this subtle change. "Did I say something wrong?" she asked.

His eyes held a touch of surprise. "It's not about being wrong," he began, hesitating. "It's just... when people know who I am, all they see is my family and their money. I'd rather be seen for who I am."

Sienna's lips quirked, her gaze drifting over to where a cluster of women seemed to cast longing glances in Dylan's direction. "You don't seem to mind attention from the ladies though," she teased, gesturing towards his 'fan club'.

Dylan turned his head in the direction she showed, a wry smile curling his lips. "That's different. Momentary distractions," he said, his tone light but with a hint of underlying seriousness.

After taking a deep breath and bolstered by a surge of unexpected boldness, she chuckled, and continued. "Well, Mr. Whitmore," she emphasized the formal title again for effect, "how about we find a quieter place? Somewhere your... distractions," she borrowed his word, "won't reach?"

There was nothing left to lose, and sometimes, taking a chance made all the difference.

The moment Dylan's fingers wrapped around Sienna's, a current of warmth shot through her, making her heart race. They weaved through the party. Her thoughts were a whirlwind of emotions. The weight of his hand in hers, the texture of his skin against her fingers; it was intoxicating. The reality that he was a Whitmore, and the warnings of Maya, echoed in the background, but for now, she was captivated by the man leading her.

When they reached the secluded garden area, the cacophony of the party melted away. The evening's symphony of crickets and rustling leaves took its place, lending a more intimate ambiance to their escape. Lanterns hung low, illuminating the pathway with their soft, golden light, dancing with the gentle breeze.

They stood beneath a canopy of wisteria, its purple blossoms cascading around them. Dylan's fingers loosened, but rather than let go, he drew her against him. The surrounding atmosphere thickened with desire. She could feel the heat radiating from him, the solidness of his chest pressed against hers. His head lowered, lips a hair's breadth from her own, and for a dizzying moment, she was sure they would kiss.

The rapid rhythm of her heart echoed in her ears, and each shallow breath was laced with his scent—a beguiling mix of earthy musk and fresh pine. It intoxicated her, blurring the lines between caution and craving. The glint in his eyes suggested he was well-versed in this dance of seduction. Sienna's thoughts wandered, imagining the path this could take, the electrifying journey they might embark upon together in this hidden corner.

Just as the tension between them grew to an almost unbearable point, a sudden chill swept through the garden. Sienna felt it—a whisper of cold that didn't belong on this summer night, accompanied by a faint rustle that didn't come from the trees. She saw Dylan stiffen, his eyes darting around as if looking for the source of the disturbance.

"Did you feel that?" Sienna asked, her voice almost a whisper.

He nodded, breaking their intimate stance. "It felt... off, didn't it?"

A chuckle escaped her lips, and he joined her, the tension dissipating. "Perhaps the spirits of White Pine don't approve of our escapade," she teased.

Dylan grinned, but it didn't quite reach his eyes. "Or maybe they just want to join the party."

Sienna let out a hearty laugh. "You know," she began, tucking a stray strand of hair behind her ear, "I've always been fascinated by the paranormal. Ghosts, spirits, unexplained phenomena—it all draws me in."

"Really?" Dylan raised an eyebrow, his face unreadable. "You believe in all that?"

She nodded. "It's not so much about believing, but about being open to the mysteries of the world. There's so much we don't understand. Why not entertain the possibility?"

He paused, letting her words sink in. "White Pine has its share of tales," he began, his voice low and cryptic. "Many are steeped in history, and some... some bear the weight of the Whitmore name."

Sienna grinned, "See? Now you're getting it."

They continued to talk, the barriers between them lowered. "You know, being a Whitmore isn't all it's cracked up to be," Dylan confessed, his gaze focused on a distant point. "People often see the name, the legacy, and the wealth. But they don't see me—the real me."

She observed him for a moment. "You want to be seen for who you are, not just your last name."

Dylan met her gaze, his eyes sincere. "Exactly. Everyone assumes they know my life because of my family name. But there's so much more to me than just being a Whitmore."

Sienna tilted her head, studying him. "People often see only what's on the surface, but we all have depths waiting to be explored," she murmured.

"I'm not used to this," he admitted. "Being candid. It's... new."

Sienna looked up at him, her gaze steady. "Maybe it's time for some new experiences, Mr. Whitmore."

He chuckled, "Only if you promise to call me Dylan from now on."

The moonlight streamed through the leaves overhead, casting silvery patterns on the path, and they settled onto a stone bench.

Sienna hesitated for a moment, sensing a shift in the atmosphere. "I realized we haven't formally introduced ourselves," she began, extending a hand. "I'm Sienna Avery, college student, and nature lover."

Dylan chuckled, accepting her hand. His grip was firm, yet warm. "Dylan Whitmore."

Sienna raised an eyebrow. "Anything more to add, Dylan?"

He grinned, "Well, aside from the obvious 'rich guy' stereotype, I have aspirations, too."

She leaned in, curiosity piqued. "Do tell."

With a dramatic sigh, he replied, "Future eco-resort tycoon?" At her confused look, he continued, "Jokes aside, I genuinely want to transform White Pine. There's so much potential here. Instead of just being another luxury destination, I want it to be a sustainable haven. The resort will cater to eco-travelers, focusing on conservation. It's high time we tread lightly on this Earth, even in the world of opulence."

Her eyes lit up. "That sounds amazing. And from my future perspective as a travel writer," she said, emphasizing the word future, "that's a story I'd love to cover."

"A travel writer, eh?" Dylan looked pleased. "See? And here I was thinking our only common interest was sneaking around in dimly lit gardens."

After that, their conversation flowed. Sienna regaled him with her college escapades and her insatiable wanderlust, her dream of exploring every nook and cranny of the world. "Each place tells a story, you know? I want to be a part of that, even if it's just for a while."

Dylan listened, rapt. He then delved into his own life - a contrast of luxury, privilege, but also of heavy expectations and responsibilities. "Your world sounds so free," he remarked, a hint of longing in his voice. "Mine's...well, it's complicated."

She reached out and plucked some wisteria from a section marked as protected. With a triumphant grin, she tucked the flower behind her ear.

Dylan arched an eyebrow, amusement in his eyes. "Breaking the rules already, Miss Avery?"

She shot him a defiant look, her lips curling into a smile. "Sometimes, you need to bend the rules to truly experience life, Mr. Whitmore," she responded, emphasizing his formal title.

His laughter echoed in the quiet garden, the harmonious notes resonating in the stillness. Their eyes met and held, the world around them blurring into a hazy background. It was as if the universe conspired to draw them closer in that singular, magical moment.

The faint strains of music from the main event wafted over, a gentle reminder of the world outside their cocoon. Without breaking their gaze, Dylan rose and extended a hand toward Sienna, his fingers outstretched. "Care to dance?"

Sienna, surprised by the unexpected request, felt a rush of warmth spread from her cheeks to her toes. With a shy smile, she took his hand, and as their fingers intertwined. A jolt of electricity coursed through her. Those storybook descriptions of 'sparks' felt all too real.

He led her to an open space in the garden, and they moved to the soft rhythm of the distant music. Their dance begun with the formal steps of a waltz, their bodies maintaining a courteous distance. But as the minutes passed, and as they grew more attuned to each other's movements and emotions, the formality faded. The space between them shrank. Their steps became less structured, more intuitive, guided by the rhythm of their heartbeats and the melody that enveloped them.

Sienna felt the world receding. Dylan's hand was on the small of her back, and the firm yet gentle grip of his fingers, and the reassuring weight of his other hand holding hers, sent shivers down her spine.

The boundaries blurred. Was it the music guiding their movements or their shared pulse? Time seemed to stand still. With every turn, every sway, they drew closer, two souls entwined in a dance as old as time. And in that moment, beneath the canopy of stars and amidst the fragrant blossoms, Sienna felt alive, her heart dancing its own joyous rhythm.

Dylan's fingers traced delicate, mesmerizing circles on the small of her back, each swirl sending tiny ripples of sensation across her skin. Sienna's pulse quickened, every nerve ending alert and responsive. Meanwhile, his other hand cradled her face, his thumb tracing the soft outline of her cheek. Their faces inched closer.

Just as their lips were mere millimeters apart, a deliberate cough shattered the intimate bubble. Startled, they pulled apart to find an older gentleman standing a few paces away on the garden path. Sienna's eyes darted to the figure, recognizing in his features a refined, mature version of the man beside her.

His silvered hair was brushed back, revealing sharp, piercing eyes that held an uncanny resemblance to Dylan's. The same chiseled jaw, the same regal bearing, but with lines etched by time and responsibility. It was unmistakable; this was an elder Whitmore. The interruption pressed on the atmosphere, a palpable tension hanging in the air.

"Father," Dylan's voice took on a more formal tone.

"Dylan," the elder Whitmore began, his voice laced with an ice-cold calmness that only years of cultivated control could achieve, "This is the season's first major event, and it would be wise for you to remember your role here. You should be at the forefront, visible, not tucked away in some shadowy nook indulging in... distractions."

His gaze shifted to Sienna, sweeping her up and down in a brief, evaluative manner. "Miss," he nodded, a curt gesture of acknowledgment, but devoid of warmth, "I trust you'll continue to enjoy the evening's festivities." It wasn't a suggestion.

Sienna took in a deep breath, fighting the flush creeping up her cheeks. She gave a small nod. "Of course, Mr. Whitmore." Her voice maintained a respectful steadiness.

As the elder Whitmore turned to leave, Dylan caught Sienna's gaze. Unspoken words hung between them. Just before they were out of sight, Dylan mouthed, "Find me later."

Sienna watched as they retreated, their silhouettes fading into the grandeur of White Pine Resorts. She took a moment to regroup, her emotions a whirlwind. There was annoyance at Dylan's swift acquiescence to his father's demand, but a part of her understood. Their worlds, she realized, were vast galaxies apart. Yet, amidst the vastness, they'd found a shared star. She stood, lost in her thoughts, the surreal nature of the evening sinking in. The connection she had felt, that undeniable spark. Was it just a fleeting moment, or the start of something more profound? Only time would tell.

Sienna made her way back to the main event, the night air cooling the warmth in her cheeks. The soft sounds of the party grew louder, and as she approached, she was swallowed by the glow of lanterns and the hum of chatter.

"Where on earth have you been?!" Maya's voice cut through. She appeared beside Sienna, a champagne flute in hand.

Sienna laughed. "Exploring, I guess. And you? Enjoying the evening?"

Maya rolled her eyes. "Danced with a few cute guys. Had some drinks. You know, the usual party routine." She paused, taking a sip from her flute. "But you seem to have been busy with Whitmore royalty. Word travels fast, Sienna."

Sienna felt a small pang of discomfort. "It's not like that, Maya. We just talked."

Maya's demeanor shifted to a more serious tone. "Look, Si, I've seen enough summer flings come and go here. Dylan's... complicated. Just be careful, okay?"

Before Sienna could respond, a familiar voice resonated behind her. "May I have this dance?"

Both women turned to find Dylan, looking as handsome as ever, extending his hand towards Sienna. The urgency in his eyes was unmistakable. Maya shot Sienna a look and retreated, leaving the two of them in their own bubble once more.

Sienna hesitated for just a beat before accepting. As Dylan took her hand, he slipped a folded piece of paper into her palm. The unexpected gesture surprised her, and their eyes met with a shared secret. Without a word, she tucked the paper into her bra.

The music enveloped them as they moved together. This time, there was a tender familiarity in their dance, a mutual understanding that something deeper was unfolding between them.

No words were exchanged when their dance concluded. Throughout the rest of the night, Dylan mingled with other attendees, dancing and laughing, but his eyes often strayed back to Sienna, seeking her out amidst the crowd. Every glance felt like a secret shared between them, a connection they couldn't ignore.

Sienna stationed herself beside Maya, enjoying the rest of the evening with light chatter and soft laughter. They shared stories, observations, and the occasional playful gossip about the other party-goers.

As the night aged, the energy of the party waned. The live music dwindled to softer tunes, guests began their departures, and soon enough, Sienna and Maya made the walk back to their respective rooms.

Once inside her room, the buzz of excitement from the party still lingering in her veins, Sienna pulled the crinkled piece of paper from her bra. She unfolded it, revealing a number, Dylan's. Without overthinking it, she typed out a message: "It's Sienna. I had a wonderful time with you tonight." She pressed send and waited, but no response came.

Around her, the room was alive with her roommates' giggles and recounting of their own evening escapades.

They were animated, their voices blending into a backdrop of chatter. Sienna tuned them out, her mind preoccupied with her own evening.

She crawled into her bed, the cool sheets enveloping her. As the soft murmurs of the night continued around her, she found herself deep in thought. The electric connection with Dylan, Maya's warning, the cryptic exchange of numbers — it was all so thrilling yet so perplexing. The potential of a summer romance was tantalizing, but the complexities it promised made her wonder: Was it worth it? With that thought lingering in her mind, Sienna's eyelids grew heavy, and she succumbed to a dream-filled sleep.

CHAPTER THREE

Rain-Kissed Revelations

White Pine Resort glistened in the early morning light, its beauty enhanced by the misty haze. As the days had gone by, Sienna had grown more comfortable in her role at the resort. Today, the scent of fresh linens mingled with the faint aroma of breakfast cooking somewhere in the distance. Nearby, the gentle clinking of dishes created a soft backdrop, setting the pace for the day ahead.

Sienna settled into the rhythm of the day, handling her tasks effortlessly. As she went about her duties, her eyes drifted, scanning the faces of guests and staff. She was looking for one person in particular. Dylan had been missing since the party, leaving her to wonder if their encounter had been nothing more than a mere distraction for him.

Friday had arrived with a sense of urgency. As soon as Sienna started her shift, she was swept up in the whirlwind of work, the resort alive with activity. The hours melded together in a hectic mix of tasks, guests, and brief moments of calm. Before she knew it, her shift supervisor signaled it was time for her break; lunchtime had crept up on her. The morning's frenzy had flown by in a flash.

In the bustling lunchroom, Sienna joined Maya and Jess, a fellow summer worker who served in the resort's upscale restaurant. Jess animatedly recounted tales of eccentric guest requests, her hands illustrating each story, drawing laughter from those around. After sharing a few of her own experiences, Maya leaned in, her voice dropping to a hush. "Have you heard? There's talk that the Whitmores might spend more time here this season. Rumor has it that someone in the family is sick, maybe with cancer. But nothing's confirmed yet."

Jess rolled her eyes, her voice laced with mock exasperation. "Just what we need—more Whitmores to entertain." As she said this, her gaze flickered toward Sienna, the unspoken words clear in her expression.

Sienna played coy. "Oh, speaking of Whitmores, is Dylan still around?"

Maya smirked, taking a sip of her drink. "Hoping for a little more quality time with Dylan?"

Before Sienna could even get a word out, Jess jumped in, rolling her eyes and saying in a grave tone, "Seriously? Why even bother? Word on the street is he's just here playing the rich boy role, waiting until he's called back to his fancy palace or whatever."

Sienna shrugged, trying to mask her curiosity. "We just had a… moment. I'm intrigued, that's all."

Jess leaned in closer, lowering her voice. "Look, I've been around this block a few times. Just watch yourself with the Whitmores, especially that Dylan guy. Guys like him? They pop in, stir things up and then jet. It's all fun and games for them, but it's the rest of us who end up dealing with the drama they leave behind."

Sienna looked back at Jess with a half-smile. "I hear you, Jess. But I can take care of myself, okay?"

Jess shrugged, "Whatever." She then quickly changed the subject, her eyes lighting up. "Anyway, did you hear about the new chef they're bringing in next week? I heard he's worked all over the world!"

Sienna savored the last bites of her sandwich, enjoying the brief respite her midday break provided from the morning's chaos. As she sat in the resort's sunlit cafeteria, the hum of conversations filled the air—employees discussing their tasks, guests, and the evening's upcoming events.

As she listened, Sienna picked up on a mix of stories about the Whitmores. Some people praised them for their smart business moves and charity work, while others dished about the family's more scandalous moments. Gossip spread about secret romances, shady business deals, and wild nights out, especially involving the younger Whitmores. And, of course, with Dylan being the heir and a bit of a mystery, he was often the star of these hushed conversations.

As she sipped her iced tea, lost in her thoughts, Maya pulled her back to the present moment.. "You look like you've run a marathon," Maya commented, noting Sienna's tired eyes.

"It feels like it," Sienna replied with a weary smile. "These Friday check-ins are no joke."

Maya nodded. "It's always a madhouse. But you're doing great. By midsummer, you'll be breezing through it."

Their chat moved on to everyday stuff, but Sienna didn't miss the quick look Maya shot Ben's way. Ah, Ben. He was funny, always had a witty comeback, and seemed to be everywhere. They'd danced at the party and bumped into each other a few times during the week. Sienna liked his straightforwardness, especially when he dropped ob-

vious hints about Dylan. But dancing with Ben felt just...
nice, lacking the electric connection she felt with Dylan.

Ben, sensing Sienna's gaze, looked up from his table
across the room and sent a playful wink her way. She responded with a smile, noting the slight hint of hopefulness
in his eyes.

As they started clearing their lunch trays and getting
ready to head back to work, Sienna couldn't help but get
caught up in her thoughts about Dylan. Was what she felt
was just a one-off thing because of that night, or was there
something real there?

After pushing the door open, she stepped back into the
fray. The lobby buzzed with activity, the sound of rolling
suitcases, and the constant chime of the reception bell. It
was going to be a long day.

Fridays were always hectic at White Pine Resort, but
this one topped the charts. A flood of check-ins had the
place buzzing—families, couples, and solo adventurers all
eager to soak up a weekend in the majestic mountains.
Each guest brought not only their luggage, but a flurry of
requests and tasks that Sienna and her team scrambled to
handle.

She spent the day escorting guests to their rooms,
fielding an endless stream of questions, and making sure
every tiny detail upheld the resort's exacting standards. By

evening, her feet throbbed, her voice rasped, and a dull ache pulsed in her temples. Toss in the emotional roller-coaster of dealing with Ben and Maya, not to mention her thoughts swirling around Dylan, and it felt like she'd lived a week in just one day.

Exhausted, Sienna trudged to her dorm, each step heavy with fatigue. See closed the door behind and collapsed onto her bed. A mix of excitement, doubt, and anticipation stirred inside her, leaving her to wonder if she was truly prepared for whatever lay ahead.

Pulling her laptop close, Sienna plunged into the shadowy lore of the frozen tears trail. Her screen flickered with accounts of chilling events and spectral figures that had been sighted weaving through the misty woods. As she absorbed an old tale, a sudden chill brushed against her, as if someone had settled next to her on the bed. She spun around, heart racing, only to find nothing there. A shiver ran down her spine as she shook off the feeling and refocused on the eerie stories before her. She had always let her imagination get the best of her.

As night deepened, thoughts of Dylan occasionally drifted through her mind—his intense gaze, the undeniable spark between them. It had felt almost otherworldly, and she half-expected him to appear, perhaps to join her on a nighttime adventure along the haunted trail. Yet, a week had passed without a glimpse of him. Sienna accepted that their encounter might have been just a fleeting thing.

Sienna leaned back into her bed and exhaled slowly. A fling with Dylan might not have been so bad, she pondered. No complications, just the pleasure of his company. But for now, the mysteries of the trail captured her intrigue. The allure of unraveling the unknown called to her. It pulled her thoughts away from what might have been and into the shadows of what awaited her in the haunted woods.

Tucked under her covers, the dim glow from her phone lit up. A notification flickered on the screen—it was a message from Dylan. He texted just as her thoughts had drifted away from him. Typical, that's just how the universe works.

"Hey Sienna. Hope you've been well. Been a bit caught up with family stuff recently."

She typed back, "Hey Dylan. I've noticed you've been MIA. Everything okay on the family front?"

He responded, "You could say it's the usual Whitmore family drama. Thanks for asking. How's the job treating you?"

Sienna's fingers danced over her phone's keyboard. "Busy, especially Fridays. But I'm getting the hang of it.

Met some cool people too. Though I've heard a fair bit of… rumors about the Whitmores."

Dylan's reply came with a hint of humor. "Haha, we're kind of infamous in these parts. Not all of it's true, just so you know. How's your week looking ahead?"

She took a moment to frame her response. "Working straight through to Sunday. But I've got Monday and Tuesday off. I've made plans for Monday, but how about catching up on Tuesday?"

A few minutes of anticipation went by before his message came in. "Tuesday might be possible. Let me see how things pan out on my end. I'll get back to you."

Sienna smiled as she replied, "Sounds good. Let me know. And don't be a stranger."

His last message for the night was reassuring. "Promise I won't. Goodnight, Sienna."

She typed back with a soft sigh, "Goodnight, Dylan."

Sienna held her phone close, the glow from their conversation dimming. She felt a tug of conflicting emotions. Alone in her bed, amidst the occasional giggles and murmurs from her roommates, she wished for a space of her own. With a sigh, she turned to her side and wrapped herself around her pillow, seeking comfort and warmth as she drifted into a restless slumber.

It was Monday morning, and Sienna stood at the entrance of the Frozen Tears Trail. The days leading up to this had been a blur of activity—preparations, shifts at the resort, eager guests, and whispered rumors. Today, her backpack weighed on her shoulders as a thick mist swirled around her ankles, giving the trail an air of ancient mystery. The crisp morning air filled her lungs, invigorating and calming her at the same time.

The world of White Pine Resort had vanished behind her. Now, surrounded by the embrace of dense forest, Sienna stepped over roots and stones, her ears tuned to the chirps of birds and the murmur of a hidden stream. Each breath drew in the crisp air, mingling the scents of pine and earth. She paused, a shiver of excitement running through her as the forest whispered its ancient stories. The legends seemed to rise from the shadowed corners and thick undergrowth.

Sienna pressed on, the soft earth giving way under her boots. Each step intertwined her deeper with the natural world, every breath drawing in stories of love, betrayal, and restless spirits that had drawn her to this trail on her precious day off.

As she ventured further, ancient markers and symbols carved into rocks marked the haunting history of the trail. Each etching was like discovering a new chapter of the trail's saga, and Sienna delighted in piecing together its mysteries. From the tragic tale of a young woman named Eliza to the mysteries of those who disappeared without a trace. The stories were so vivid she could swear she saw shadows darting between the trees.

Meanwhile, thoughts of Dylan crept into her mind. Tentative plans had been made for Sienna and Dylan to meet for coffee at the resort the next day. They had only exchanged a few texts, and Sienna couldn't help but wonder if he would even show up.

Before long, the path led her into a dreamy clearing. Golden sunlight filtered through the trees, casting dappled patterns on the ground. She paused, captivated by the serenity and the nearby stream. It was a snapshot moment, one she wished she could hold on to a little longer.

As she sipped from her water bottle, a rustle from the bushes caused her to freeze in place. Her pulse quickened, and for a split second, the ghostly legends associated with the trail flashed through her mind. Could it be? She turned her head toward the sound, bracing herself. Instead, as the foliage parted, a familiar pair of blue eyes met hers, reflecting an equal measure of surprise.

"Dylan?" Sienna stammered, incredulous.

He stepped out, looking disarmed. "Sienna? What are you doing here?" He laughed, brushing a hand through his tousled hair. "Not that I'm complaining."

She chuckled, shaking her head. "I could ask you the same thing. I thought you'd be busy with... whatever it is the Whitmores do."

He grinned. "Needed a break from the world. You?"

"Same." She smiled. "Plus, I've wanted to hike this trail since I got here. Heard a lot about its legends."

"That's right, you had an interest in the supernatural." Dylan's gaze swept across the clearing, landing on Sienna. He held her eyes and murmured, "It's beautiful."

A faint blush tinged Sienna's cheeks, uncertain if he was talking about the trail or something more. The intensity of his stare made her heart flutter. A comfortable silence settled between them, punctuated only by the babbling of the stream and the occasional chirp of a bird. Then, with a playful smirk, Sienna broke the silence. "So, did you follow me here?"

He raised an eyebrow, feigning indignation. "Now, why would I do that? Maybe it's you who followed me."

Sienna laughed, the sound echoing in the clearing. "Oh, so it's like that, is it?"

Dylan's face softened, and he took a step closer, his voice dropping to a whisper. "Honestly, this feels like one of those cosmic jokes. Of all the trails, at all the times..."

She looked up into his eyes, the depth of their blue even more pronounced in the daylight. "It does feel like the universe is playing some sort of game with us, doesn't it?"

He nodded, and for a moment, they stood there, lost in each other's gaze, the weight of the past days and their unspoken words hanging between them.

Sienna cleared her throat, the spell breaking. "Well, since you're here, and I'm here, fancy joining me for the rest of the hike?"

Dylan's smile was genuine, lighting up his face. "I thought you'd never ask."

Together, they continued along the trail, the barriers that had existed between them seeming to melt away with each step. The easy banter, the shared laughter. It all felt like they were picking up from where they'd left off. The universe might play games, but in that clearing, on that day, it felt like it was rooting for them.

The trail twisted and turned, revealing hidden gems like cascading waterfalls or panoramic viewpoints. With every step, Sienna and Dylan seemed to shed layers of their initial apprehensions and hesitations, finding comfort in the shared journey.

Dylan paused near the edge of a brook, his gaze distant, as if remembering a tale from long ago. "See that brook over there? It's named after Eliza Goodwin. The story is pretty tragic."

Sienna's eyebrows furrowed in curiosity, her attention piqued. "Tell me more about Eliza. I read about her in the brochure, but it only gave a brief mention."

"Ah," Dylan started. "Back in 1788, right here in Crawford Notch, there were two young people—Eliza, a servant, and John Swanson, a loyal farmhand. They both worked for my ancestor, Colonel Joseph Whitmore. They dreamed of running away and building a life together. Eliza managed to save up a dowry and even went back to Portsmouth to plan their wedding."

Sienna leaned in, captivated. She had read the story, but it felt like it was alive when Dylan told it. "So, what happened?"

"Colonel Whitmore persuaded John to give up his plans with Eliza and join the revolutionary forces, and took Eliza's hard-earned dowry to help fund their efforts." Dylan said, his voice growing heavier. "When Eliza found out, she rushed back from Portsmouth, intent on confronting John. In her haste, she tried to cross an icy brook and, tragically, she never made it to the other side."

"Hence the Frozen Tears..." Sienna's eyes widened in shock. "That's heartbreaking."

"There's more," Dylan whispered. "When John found out about Eliza's fate, guilt consumed him. The burden of what he had done drove him to madness."

Sienna sighed, her heart heavy. "And now, they say her spirit still lingers here?"

Dylan nodded. "Especially on cold winter nights. Some claim they hear a young woman's laughter, turning to sobs of despair." His eyes darkened. For a moment, it looked like he was going to divulge more, but then he just shut his mouth, as if catching himself. The weight of a deeper story hung in the air between them. Sienna studied his expression, sensing there was more he wasn't saying.

The story lingered in the air, and for a moment, the natural sounds of the forest seemed to hush. Bird chirps ceased, the rustle of leaves stilled, and even the water seemed to quieten. The sudden stillness was palpable, the world around them holding its breath.

Then a gentle breeze wafted through, sending a shiver down Sienna's spine. The sensation intensified, and it felt like someone was watching her. She wrapped her arms around herself, as if to ward off the sudden chill, but it wasn't just the cold that affected her. It felt as though the essence of Eliza Goodwin was present, mourning her lost love.

Dylan, too, sensed the shift. He glanced around, his eyes searching the surroundings before settling back on Sienna. "It's said that sometimes, when her story is told, she makes her presence felt," he whispered.

Sienna gulped. "It feels like she's right here with us, doesn't it?"

He nodded and stepped closer to Sienna. "You know, sometimes the past doesn't just stay in the past, especially in places like this where emotions are so deep."

The two stood close, wrapped up in the place's ambiance. After what seemed like an eternity, the forest stirred once again. Birds resumed their songs, and the gentle gurgle of the brook filled the air, bringing with it a sense of normalcy.

Sienna took a deep breath. "That was... surreal."

Dylan smiled, his eyes still reflecting the depth of the moment.

As they progressed down the trail, they found a serene spot beside a moss-draped rock near the water's edge. The streams refreshing mist cast upon their faces created a calming ambiance. Here, Dylan opened up, sharing more about his life. With every story, Sienna glimpsed a side of Dylan that was worlds away from grand events or the expectations tied to the Whitmore name.

They shared sandwiches, chuckling at the quirks of guests they'd encountered at the resort. Sienna playfully mimicked a demanding guest, causing Dylan to burst into laughter. Amid their camaraderie, sometimes their hands would accidentally brush. Each fleeting touch left her wanting more. Their eyes would meet, holding onto that shared moment a second longer than necessary.

The world around them seemed to blur. It wasn't just about the trail's mysteries anymore; it was about them, discovering each other amidst nature's embrace. At one particularly breathtaking viewpoint, they stood side by side, looking out at the expanse below. The sun's rays painted the sky in hues of gold and crimson, casting a warm glow on their faces.

Dylan broke the silence, his voice barely above a whisper, "I often come here when I need a break from... well, everything. It's like a sanctuary."

Sienna glanced sideways at him. "The resort, the parties, the expectations... It's a lot, isn't it?"

He sighed, nodding. "More than you can imagine. But out here, it all fades away."

She felt a pang of sympathy. Maybe the player rumors were just that—rumors. Perhaps beneath the facade was a soul yearning for simplicity, just like her.

As the afternoon progressed, the forest canopy and the fading sunlight wrapped them in their own secluded world. The sky, once clear and blue, gradually darkened with gathering clouds. Suddenly, a lone raindrop landed on Sienna's nose, followed by more that pattered against the surrounding leaves. What started as a few sporadic drops quickly escalated into a steady downpour, and in no time, they were caught in a full-blown storm.

Dylan glanced up, cursing softly under his breath. "Didn't think it'd rain today."

Sienna laughed, feeling the water soak through her clothes. "Neither did I. We need to find shelter."

Driven by the urgency of the situation, they scanned their surroundings. It was Dylan who spotted it first — a small cave-like alcove tucked away between massive boulders, offering a semblance of refuge from the relentless rain.

"Over there!" he pointed, and without wasting a moment, the two of them sprinted towards it. They stumbled into the shelter, gasping and dripping, their bodies pressed close together in the confined space. The sudden proximity caused Sienna's heart to race — or perhaps it was the sprint; she couldn't quite tell.

Outside, the rain continued its symphony; the sound amplified in their shelter. Each drop seemed to beat in time with Sienna's heart. Dylan's body felt warm against hers, and she turned to look at him. Their eyes locked, and for a moment, the rain, the alcove, and the world outside ceased to exist. It was just the two of them, their breaths mingling in the cool, damp air.

"I, uh..." Dylan started, his voice betraying a hint of nervousness. "I didn't expect our day to turn out quite like this."

Sienna chuckled softly, "Neither did I." She paused, her gaze dropping to his lips for a split second, then returning to his eyes. "You think Eliza's trying to tell us something?"

Dylan smirked. "Maybe she's playing matchmaker from beyond?"

Their shared laughter echoed, but beneath it, an unspoken tension simmered. As the rain continued its serenade, Sienna wondered if Dylan was feeling the same pull she was experiencing. She ventured a guess. "You know, I've always found the rain... romantic."

Dylan, with a playful tilt of his head, replied, "Is that so? Perhaps we should thank the rain then, for this unexpected moment."

In the close quarters, their shared laughter gradually faded, leaving behind a silence charged with anticipation. The dim light filtering through the curtain of rain outside cast a gentle glow on their faces, highlighting the drops of water that clung to their skin.

Dylan's look, usually playful, took on a serious intensity. He paused for just a moment before closing the gap between them.

Their lips barely touched when Sienna, swept up in the moment, shifted her stance. Unfortunately, her head collided with a low-hanging rock, abruptly ending their kiss. A surprised yelp escaped her as they both pulled back, trying not to laugh at the sudden turn of events.

Dylan pulled back, concern in his eyes. "Are you okay?"

Sienna rubbed the spot where she'd bumped her head and chuckled. "I'm fine. Just the universe's way of keeping me grounded, literally."

Dylan's laughter joined hers, easing the moment. "Seems like nature always has a knack for reminding us it's here, usually when we least expect it."

Then Dylan took her hand, intertwining their fingers, and together they shifted. They settled side by side, their shoulders touching, leaning back against the cool stone of the alcove. The silence wasn't uncomfortable; it was a shared moment of contentment and understanding. The steady rhythm of the rain became their soundtrack, each drop telling stories of moments like this—fleeting, yet unforgettable.

"You know, I've always had this privilege, this cushioned life as a Whitmore, but with it comes a cage. Walls of expectations." Dylan's eyes held a sadness, the weight of a gilded cage pressing down. "It's why I'm here, working different roles at the resort. To understand the real essence of our business, and to, well, find a bit of freedom. My grandfather... he always told me about his adventures, and I guess that's what inspired me."

Sienna nodded, the longing for freedom in his voice resonating with her own aspirations. "I grew up on my grandmother's tales. Stories of love, adventures, the beauty of nature. It's why I'm so drawn to the outdoors. My parents taught me the values of hard work and integrity. They've given up so much for me to attend college, and every day, I juggle classes with part-time jobs. But when I'm out here," she gestured at the surrounding expanse, "it feels like I can breathe. I dream of seeing the world, maybe writing about it or making documentaries."

"Documentaries?" Dylan's eyebrows lifted in genuine interest, his hand brushing a droplet from her cheek, his touch lingering longer than necessary. "That's amazing.

The world needs more authentic storytellers, people who can capture that raw essence of life."

Sienna blushed at his touch, her heart rate picking up. "It's just a dream for now," she admitted. "But every time I'm out here, it feels like a step closer to that reality."

Dylan's fingers brushed against hers. "You know, our dreams might not be so different," he mused. "I want the resort to be a place that tells stories, too. Stories of nature, of sustainability, of connection."

Their faces were close now, their breaths mingling. Sienna's eyes flickered down to his lips and then back up, a challenge and invitation all in one. "Sometimes, dreams have a way of becoming reality when we least expect them to."

With that, Dylan leaned in, capturing her lips once again, this time with a soft, lingering kiss.

As minutes passed, the intensity of the rain diminished. What started as a torrential downpour eased into a soft drizzle, then mere droplets falling from the trees.

"Seems like the storm's passing," Dylan remarked, peering out of the alcove.

She nodded, taking a deep breath, inhaling the fresh scent that always follows a rainstorm. "Let's get going," she said.

Together, they stepped out onto the damp earth, drawn by the beckoning end of the trail. The world around shimmered with droplets on leaves, and distant birdsong filled the air as they journeyed side by side.

CHAPTER FOUR

Whispers of the Past

The forest seemed alive with ancient memories, each rustling leaf and distant bird call echoing the rhythms of long-past eras. As Sienna and Dylan ventured deeper, they came upon a fork in their path—a divergence where beams of dappled sunlight broke through the thick canopy, beckoning them to explore.

However, as they approached, a sudden silence enveloped them, halting the forest sounds. It was as though time itself paused, paying homage. At the end of the side trail, there was a brook. Next to it stood an old marker, entangled in nature's grasp, its story veiled by moss and time.

Dylan, a flicker of unease in his eyes, stepped forward. He brushed aside the debris to reveal the cracked inscriptions beneath. Words like *love* and *betrayal* emerged, causing him to swallow hard, a shadow passing over his face. "I've never been here," he whispered. "This is where she died... Eliza Goodwin."

Sienna followed his gaze to the marker when suddenly, Dylan staggered back, clutching his cheek where a vivid red mark flared.

His eyes widened, a flash of recognition crossing his face, but he quickly covered it with a forced casualness. "Must've been a stray branch or something," he muttered, dismissing the incident, although the mark on his cheek suggested otherwise.

Sienna looked around, noting the absence of any trees close enough to have hit him. Then, the air grew heavy, making each breath a struggle. Wordlessly, Sienna reached for Dylan's hand. Did he feel it too? It was if time itself had grown dense. A barely noticeable breeze stirred, making Sienna shiver. She thought she felt a light touch on her hair, like a caress. Startled, she looked around, but nothing was out of place.

She hesitated a moment, her eyes searching Dylan's, then whispered, "Let's keep going."

Dylan nodded. Together, they went back to the main path; the marker continuing its silent watch over the brook, waiting for the next souls brave enough to approach.

As they distanced themselves from the scene, the forest stirred back to life. The suffocating stillness gave way to nature's chorus: leaves rustling in the breeze, the lively calls of birds overhead, and the harmonious hum of insects. Yet Sienna couldn't shake a nagging sense of unease. Now and then, she thought she heard an extra footstep or a whisper uncomfortably close.

Meanwhile, Dylan seemed captivated by the beauty, unaware of her discomfort. "Every time I come here, it feels like the first time," he said, his voice taking on a distant tone.

Sienna nodded, but her senses were on high alert. When she tried to reach out and touch Dylan, a heavy sense of foreboding gripped her heart. It was as if an unseen force was warning her, urging her to maintain her distance. She tried shaking off the feeling, attributing it to the strange marker.

"You okay?" Dylan asked.

"Yeah, just... thought I felt something," Sienna replied, trying to sound casual.

The odd sensation intensified. Sienna was almost certain she heard muted whispers, but each time she tried to locate where they were coming from, they faded away. Despite the eerie atmosphere, being near Dylan provided a measure of comfort, even though he seemed oblivious to the ghostly undertones enveloping them.

Sienna pushed her discomfort aside. "Let's keep going."

For the rest of their hike, an unspoken tension lingered, with Sienna on edge and Dylan none the wiser. As they neared the parking lot, the dense canopy thinned, giving way to the open sky. A familiar crunch of gravel under their feet announced their arrival. The area, once bustling, had quieted down, with only two cars remaining in the lot. Long shadows stretched across the ground, dancing in the soft glow of the early evening sun.

Sienna walked towards her trusty Toyota and patted its roof. "This is me," she said with a hint of pride in her voice, always valuing her self-reliance.

Her eyes darted between the cars—her older, worn-out vehicle and Dylan's shiny BMW parked just a few spaces away. The contrast was a silent reminder of the different worlds they came from. A tight knot formed in her stomach as she caught a brief shadow of discomfort cross Dylan's face before he masked it. Did he regret bringing his fancy car? Was he judging her?

Dylan's voice broke through her spiraling thoughts. "You know, there's a diner not too far from here. Ever tried it?"

Sienna, grateful for the change in topic, shook her head. "Can't say I have."

"It's a classic. Let's grab a bite? You can follow me."

As Sienna drove behind Dylan, her mind was a whirlwind of thoughts. Growing up, she had always been the one hustling—picking up extra shifts, saving for everything, wearing her independence like a badge of honor. She took pride in managing on her own, driving an older car, and skipping nights out to make ends meet.

In stark contrast, Dylan's world seemed steeped in privilege. The allure of his lifestyle was undeniable—sleek cars, sophistication, and doors that were always open. Yet, it also brewed a mix of intimidation and insecurity within her. She wondered if he could ever understand the struggle of not having everything handed to him. Would she always feel a twinge of inadequacy around him? The pressures of 'having it all' already consumed her thoughts, and being near Dylan seemed to amplify these feelings tenfold.

The drive to the diner was short but tense. Dylan's BMW took each turn while Sienna followed in her older car, her headlights occasionally catching his image in the rearview mirror. She adjusted the radio and tried to shake off the heavy thoughts about their contrasting worlds.

Soon, the diner's glowing neon sign appeared, bathing the parking lot in a warm red glow. The place had a vintage vibe, which felt comforting. Dylan parked near the entrance, and Sienna pulled in beside him, pausing a moment to collect her thoughts before getting out.

As they walked side by side to the diner, the nostalgic sounds of a classic jukebox tune welcomed them. They stepped inside, and were wrapped in the hum of sizzling grills, lively chatter, and the smell of diner classics. Dylan gestured for Sienna to choose their seats. She picked two stools at the counter, their shiny chrome reflecting the diner's charm.

"These fries are the best," Dylan said, a hint of pride in his voice. "This place is my favorite."

Sienna looked at him. "You really prefer this to the upscale places you're used to?"

Dylan laughed, brushing a hand through his hair. "Yes! Growing up, I went to boarding schools, and our main house is in New York. But I've always loved it here. I didn't come every summer, but when I did..." He swept an affectionate hand around the diner. "The mountains, the atmosphere—it's grounding. Coming here feels like reconnecting with a piece of my heart."

Sienna leaned closer. "Why is that? If it's so special, wouldn't you want to come more often?"

Dylan paused and tilted his head before speaking. "Every summer, I could choose one place to spend my vacation. Despite having tons of options, I always picked here. It was a break from the pressures of school and high expectations. One summer, after a tough term, I found this diner while sulking around town. The smell of grilled burgers pulled me in. For a few hours, I wasn't the heir to a business empire or the kid who had to be perfect; I was just a teenager enjoying a burger."

Sienna smiled. "It's amazing how places tie us to memories, isn't it? My family camped up north every summer. Not here, but the feel is the same. Story Land, hiking, campfire nights with hotdogs on sticks." She smiled, a trace of nostalgia in her voice. "One summer, when I was seven, we stayed at a campground the entire season after losing our apartment. It was tough, but those memories are precious." She paused, her eyes wandering over the diner. "I've never been here before, yet it feels linked to all those moments from my past."

Dylan met her gaze, his expression softening with understanding. "That's the magic of places like this—they're timeless. Whether it's our hundredth visit or our first, they stir up memories and help us make new ones." He grinned.

"Speaking of making memories, shall we start with those famous fries?"

The fries, golden and gleaming in a red plastic basket, beckoned. Sienna bit into one, its crispy shell giving way to the soft, flavorful potato inside. The perfect blend of salt and earthiness exploded in her mouth. She couldn't help but moan in delight. Dylan chuckled, "That good, huh?" Blushing, Sienna nodded and reached for another.

Their easy banter continued as they shared the meal, but Sienna's thoughts lingered, pondering her place in Dylan's world. Could their different paths merge, or would the contrasts always stand out?

Then she caught sight of an older woman a few booths away, observing them. Her face, etched with lines that spoke of many years, was focused. To Sienna, there was something unsettling about her stare. She couldn't help but wonder if the woman recognized something in their interaction, or if she was lost in her own memories from long ago.

It felt almost as if she was taking part in their conversation, piecing together his own narrative from their interactions. The old woman seemed to sense her observation. She approached, steps deliberate but unhurried. Sienna's heartbeat quickened, curiosity piqued.

"You two were at the old Eliza Goodwin monument earlier today, weren't you?" she inquired.

Sienna's brows knit together. "How did you know?" she asked, a touch of disbelief in her voice.

The woman smiled. "I heard you two talking about it earlier. Plus, folks who venture there always have a certain... look about them afterward."

Dylan raised an eyebrow. "We were, indeed. It's quite a spot. Have you always known about it?"

"Always?" The woman laughed. "Well, that might be stretching it a bit, but let's just say the story of that place has been a part of my family's lore for many years. I'm Mrs. Caldwell, and I've spent a fair bit of my life digging into our town's history."

Sienna's voice carried a hint of anticipation. "We sensed something... peculiar there. If you have time, we'd love to hear more about it."

Mrs. Caldwell settled onto a stool beside them. After taking a moment to collect her thoughts, she began, "You see, Eliza Goodwin wasn't just any young woman. She was fiercely independent and had dreams much larger than the constraints of her station."

Dylan and Sienna exchanged a glance as Mrs. Caldwell continued, "Working on the estate of the ambitious Colonel Joseph Whitmore, she fell in love with John

Swansonl, a farmhand with eyes as deep as the Notch's valleys. They both dreamt of a future away from the watchful eyes of the Colonel."

Her voice took on a softer, mournful tone. "To secure this dream, Eliza handed over her saved dowry to John and left for Portsmouth to plan for their new life. However, Colonel Whitmore, sensing an opportunity, convinced John to abandon Eliza and join the forces for independence, with her dowry as finance."

Sienna nodded, remembering the story.

Mr. Caldwell continued, "When Eliza found out, her heartbreak was immense. Driven by both love and a sense of betrayal, she raced back through the winter terrains. But near an icy brook, overcome by cold and despair, she made the fateful decision to cross it. She didn't survive the chilling waters."

A silence hung in the air, only broken by the low hum of the jukebox in the background.

"But that's not where the tale ends," Mrs. Caldwell added. "Learning of Eliza's tragic end, Jim was shattered. The guilt of his betrayal and her death led him to madness, and he died, tormented, in an asylum."

Dylan's voice, soft and full of emotion, broke the silence. "And the Colonel?"

Mrs. Caldwell's eyes darkened. "He might've escaped man-made justice, but they say nature has its own ways. His life, thereafter, was filled with misfortune and tragedy. Some believe it was Eliza's spirit ensuring he paid for his treachery."

Her voice dropped to a near whisper, causing Sienna and Dylan to lean in. "Some say that Eliza's spirit, in her sorrow and anger, cursed the Whitmore lineage. They say that no Whitmore shall ever find a true love that lasts, that every romance is doomed to end in heartbreak."

Sienna shot a sidelong glance at Dylan, whose face had turned a shade paler, the playful light in his eyes replaced by a shadowed darkness. He looked lost in thought, haunted by his family's past. However, he masked it, offering a tight-lipped smile to Mrs. Caldwell.

The old woman, sensing the shift, said, "But legends, they change and evolve. Curses can be broken, and destinies can be rewritten."

Sienna sighed and broke the silence, remarking, "You have a gift, Mrs. Caldwell. Ever considered being a tour guide? Your storytelling is...captivating."

"Perhaps in another life, dear." The woman chuckled, "For now, I'm content with occasional listeners like you."

Sienna's eyes were wide as she watched Mrs. Caldwell shuffle back to his booth. "That was... intense," she began.

"A curse? Dylan, do you think she knew who you are? About you being a Whitmore?"

Dylan's lips pressed into a thin line, an uncharacteristic unease flitting across his features. "It's hard to say. Maybe she just wanted to spook the city folks who wandered into her territory. The Whitmores are well known in these parts." He took a deep breath, then admitted, "But there is talk of a curse within the family. I've always taken it with a grain of salt, considering it is just a strange tale spun by the older generations."

Sienna leaned forward, intrigued. "A family curse? That's... fascinating, and kind of scary."

Dylan chuckled, trying to lighten the mood. "Every illustrious family has its skeletons, right? Perhaps ours is more... mythical. But honestly, I wouldn't worry too much about it. Mrs. Caldwell probably just has a flair for theatrics."

Sienna played with the straw in her drink, deep in thought. "It's strange," she began, "how some stories seem to transcend time. That story of Eliza and John... it felt personal, as if we've lived it before."

Dylan looked thoughtful. "You mean like... destiny?"

She nodded. "Maybe. It's as if our paths, like theirs, are intertwined by something larger than just chance. A cosmic pull, maybe."

Dylan studied her. "That's a heavy thought, Sienna. But it's beautiful, too. Do you believe in fate?"

She hesitated, then whispered, "I didn't use to. But with everything that's happened, I'm wondering if there are forces at play beyond our understanding. I just... I hope our story has a different ending than Eliza's and John's. And it's one filled with happiness, not heartbreak."

Dylan reached across the table and squeezed her hand. "Me too, Sienna. And if there's one thing I've learned, it's that we have the power to write our own story, no matter the family curses or old tales we've heard."

Sienna smiled, feeling lighter from his words, though the stories and omens of the past still echoed quietly in the back of her mind.

As they left the diner, the rain from earlier had given way to a clear sky. Stars peppered across the inky black night and Sienna took a deep breath, the crispness of the air filling her lungs. However, amid the peace, a sudden chill enveloped her, as if an icy finger had traced the length of her spine.

She stopped and glanced around, attempting to source the cause of the feeling. At the edge of the diner's parking lot, a shadow darted — so quick and indistinct that she questioned if it was a trick of the light or her imagination playing games with her. She remembered the tale from earlier and her experience on the trail, and couldn't help but wonder if it was Eliza's spirit. Was she being warned? Protected? Or was the spirit curious, seeking a connection in their shared experiences of love's intoxicating pull?

Sienna turned to find Dylan watching her, a hint of concern in his eyes. "You okay?" he asked.

She hesitated before answering, choosing not to voice her unsettling thoughts. "Yeah, just lost in thought. The tale from earlier was... a lot."

Dylan stepped closer, his proximity offering warmth and a sense of security. "Legends have a way of lingering, especially when they're tied to real emotions," he murmured, his voice a soothing balm to her jumbled nerves.

The intensity of his gaze drew her in, the world narrowing to just the two of them. They gravitated closer, their lips inching toward one another. Their kiss was soft, holding the promise of many more shared moments.

Dylan pulled away and brushed a stray strand of hair behind Sienna's ear. "Goodnight, Sienna," he whispered, leaving the words unsaid but understood — there was more to come between them.

With a last lingering glance, Sienna made her way to her car. As she drove away, the shadows and uncertainties of the evening faded, replaced by the warmth of that kiss and the promise of the days to come. But deep down, the chill she'd felt outside the diner remained, a quiet reminder of the mysteries that surrounded them.

After the eerie vibe of the evening and the nostalgic feel of the diner, her dorm room seemed both comforting and strange at the same time.

She shrugged off her jacket and kicked off her shoes before crawling into bed. Outside, the world was peaceful, bathed in soft moonlight—a sharp contrast to the whirlwind of emotions swirling inside her.

She had just settled under her covers, the cool sheets enveloping her tired body, when the soft ping of a text message broke the silence. Sienna grabbed her phone from the bedside table and opened it to find a message from Dylan.

Hey, just wanted to make sure you got home safe.

The warmth that spread through her was immediate and comforting.

Home and all tucked in. Thanks for checking.

There was a brief pause before another message from Dylan popped up.

So... heard of the Lost Pond Trail?

She raised an eyebrow, intrigued. *Another trail? You're full of surprises.*

His response came quick. *Wait till you hear the legends surrounding this one. Thought it might be our next adventure?*

She grinned, typing back, *You trying to scare me with another ghost story?*

Maybe. Or maybe just looking for another excuse to spend time with you, he replied.

The fluttering in her stomach intensified. After taking a breath, she typed, *Will I see you during the week at the resort?*

Dylan's reply took a little longer this time. *Things are hectic, but we're still on for coffee tomorrow, right?*

Definitely, she responded, heart pounding.

Goodnight, Sienna, he texted.

Goodnight, Dylan, she replied, placing her phone back on the bedside table.

After turning off her lamp, Sienna settled deeper into her pillows. While the shadows of Eliza's legend and the unexpected encounters of the day played in her mind, the most persistent thought was the developing bond between her and Dylan. The summer had presented her with mysteries and adventures, but the most tantalizing prospect of all was the deepening connection she felt with him.

CHAPTER FIVE

Promises in Twilight

Sienna woke up refreshed, her mind still replaying the delightful moments of her adventure. Eager to start the day, she laced up her shoes for a morning walk around the grounds. The crisp air and quiet paths provided a perfect backdrop for her thoughts, which were filled with the anticipation of meeting Dylan again.

Birdsongs filled the air, creating a natural melody while dewdrops sparkled on the leaves, painting the scene with a touch of early morning magic. Sienna inhaled, relishing the crisp, cool air and the peaceful solitude around her.

Her tranquility was interrupted by the buzz of her phone, but seeing Dylan's name flash across the screen quickened her pulse and brought a flush to her cheeks. The message that followed chilled her excitement to dismay. "Sienna, I'm truly sorry. I can't meet this morning. Family obligations. I hope you can understand."

She froze for a moment, surprised by the sudden shift in her emotions. Anger bubbled up inside. Was his wealthy background allowing him to set the terms of their relationship? Was she just a passing fancy in his privileged life?

Trying to keep her composure, she typed back, "Of course. Just let me know when you're available."

His reply was quick and non-committal. "Thank you for understanding. We'll reconnect soon."

This did little to calm her swirling thoughts. As Sienna reflected on the exchange, a whisper brushed past her ears—a sigh that seemed to echo with sorrows. The momentary pause left her shivering, prompting her to continue walking. The sun, which had seemed so welcoming earlier, now felt cold, mirroring the sudden gap that had opened up between Dylan and herself. Could she really find a place in his world, or was she destined to always feel just out of reach?

This emotional churning only intensified her sense of dislocation since the hike. Though the resort maintained its daily cadence, an uncanny haze consumed her nights. The legends of Eliza Goodwin seemed to resonate within her, echoes of the past clamoring for attention.

Since the day Dylan canceled their morning plans, Sienna's fascination with the Eliza Goodwin legend had deepened into a full-blown obsession. As days turned into weeks, she spent her free time hunched over a computer in the resort's business center. She dove into the mysteries of New Hampshire's history circa 1778. Under the harsh glow of the computer screens, Sienna sifted through articles, historical records, and any references she could find.

Her focus soon shifted towards understanding the experiences of women during the Revolutionary War. The stories she discovered highlighted their resilience and fortitude amidst great hardship. Women of that era were often confined within rigid societal roles—caring for families, maintaining homes, and tending to wounded soldiers. These examples of survival and courage moved Sienna, fueling her determination to uncover more about Eliza's life.

However, the more she delved into the past, the more it intertwined with her present. Sleepless nights became the norm as the history she had read infiltrated her dreams. She envisioned women in period attire, heard the march of soldiers' boots, and the distant beat of war drums. These dreams often left her waking up with a racing heart, overwhelmed by desperation, as though she had experienced those turbulent times herself.

Her relentless pursuit was taking a toll on her. Dark circles formed under her eyes, and her usual energy dimmed. Concerned comments from resort staff and her new friends became frequent, noting her worn-out appearance. But Sienna was too captivated by the past to heed them. She felt an unbreakable connection to Eliza's story, a bond that pulled her deeper into history, unable to detach even if she wanted to.

One evening, after they had finished their dinner, Sienna and Maya took a stroll along the winding pathways. They chatted, enjoying the cool night air and the crunch of gravel beneath their feet. Their conversation reflected the strong connection they had developed over the past few weeks.

"You seem distant," Maya remarked.

Sienna hesitated, her eyes lingering on the path ahead. "It's just this place. Adjusting to everything is... challenging."

Not convinced, Maya nudged, "It's not something about Dylan, is it?"

"No, it's not about Dylan," Sienna responded, her tone betraying a touch of fatigue. "He's complicated, yes, but I've let him go."

Maya looked at Sienna. "You haven't been sleeping well. I can tell."

A weary smile played on Sienna's lips. "Is it that obvious?" she sighed. "I'm just caught up in something, I think. But thank you, Maya. It's kind of you to be concerned."

As the pair continued along the resort's walkways, a sudden, unseasonably cold gust of wind seemed to sweep through the area. Out of the corner of her eye, Sienna glimpsed a shadowy figure near an old oak tree. But just as quickly as it had appeared, it vanished.

Sienna stopped to tie her shoelace, attempting to hide her startled reaction and using the moment to collect herself.

Maya, waiting and oblivious to the ghostly presence, remarked, "That was cold! Odd for a summer evening."

Sienna forced a light laugh. "Yeah, probably just a freak New England weather thing."

Her heart raced, but she tried to play it cool. Despite her effort, she couldn't stop herself from casting quick glances around, half-expecting to see the apparition again. Everything around them, however, remained peaceful, bathed in the soft twilight. She kept her concerns to herself, trying not to worry Maya.

Sienna's nights were filled with restlessness. In her dreams, a haunting lullaby—melancholic and ancient—wove tales of deep love and loss. When she woke, she'd scan for the source of the music, only to find the quiet room.

During the day, she felt an unseen presence accompany her near water features like fountains or brooks. Sometimes, she'd feel a gentle touch on her arm or hear a sigh carried on the breeze, as if a spirit was trying to share its sorrow with her.

These supernatural encounters blurred her sense of reality. Sipping morning coffee, she'd half expect to see her cup shrouded in mist. The gardens now seemed to host shifting shadows that flickered at the edge of her vision.

"Is this all in my head?" Sienna whispered to herself, looking into a mirror for answers. Her reflection showed weary eyes filled with confusion. And as she voiced her fears, a mournful sigh seemed to fill the room, echoing her inner turmoil.

The next day, as Sienna walked down the corridor to begin her shift, her footsteps rang out on the polished stone. Her thoughts were elsewhere when an unexpected grip encircled her waist. Her breath hitched, a scream bubbling up but never escaping, as she was quickly whisked sideways into the shadows of an empty banquet hall.

The glow from the ornate chandeliers cast a soft light on Dylan's face as he gazed into Sienna's eyes and drew her closer. She had all but written him off, but as he kissed her, the surprise gave way to a rush of emotions. For a brief instant, everything else blurred away, their connection becoming the only thing that mattered.

As his hands touched the small of her back, Sienna felt a shiver run through her, torn between the thrill of his touch and annoyance at herself for letting him get to her again. Just as she lost herself in the moment, he pulled away. Regret, perhaps even a hint of pain, flickered in his eyes before he turned and disappeared through a side door.

Sienna stood there, trying to catch her breath, her hand touching her lips. The encounter left her in a daze as she slowly made her way to start her shift.

Throughout the day, Sienna moved mechanically, serving guests and managing her tasks. Her mind kept drifting back. She was annoyed with herself for being so affected by him.

Every hallway, every doorway, every hidden corner of the resort became a place of possibility. She glanced over her shoulder at the slightest hint of a footstep, hoping and dreading in equal measure Dylan would appear. She could almost feel the pull of his presence, imagining his fingers brushing against her, or his gaze as he watched her from afar. Every unexpected touch or shadowed figure had her heart racing.

It kept her in an almost perpetual state of distraction. The war within her was tumultuous—she couldn't decide if she wanted to confront him or never see him again.

Her inattentiveness did not go unnoticed. "Sienna," the day manager said, pulling her aside mid-shift, "This isn't like you. Is everything okay? You've been off all day."

The reprimand snapped her back to reality. The fog she had been in cleared, replaced by responsibilities and the repercussions of her distraction. She murmured an apology, trying to ground herself and focus on the job. But no matter how hard she tried, she couldn't get Dylan out of her head.

After her shift, Sienna headed to the cafeteria. The room was bustling with activity. Groups of her colleagues gathered together, chatting in lively tones. But as Sienna approached, the atmosphere changed. Conversations turned into hushed whispers. She could feel the eyes on her..

"Sienna! Over here!" Maya called. Sienna made her way to where her friend sat, relieved to see a friendly face.

Maya's gaze probed her face. "You okay?" she asked, nudging a cup of tea toward Sienna.

After taking a deep breath, Sienna nodded. "I'm fine. Just another day, I guess."

There was a pause, one filled with the unspoken, before Maya ventured further. "People have been talking...

about you and Dylan. Someone saw you two together." Her voice trailed off, her eyes full of questions. "And given the Whitmores' reputation, well... they're all wondering how it's going to play out."

Sienna's heart skipped a beat. She had hoped the stolen moment would remain theirs alone, but in a place like this, there were no secrets. She met Maya's eyes. "It was just... a kiss. Nothing more." But even as she said it, she wondered if she was trying to convince Maya or herself.

Before Sienna could process this, Ben sauntered over. "Sienna," he began, fixing her with a meaningful look, "is it true? Are you and Dylan...you know?"

She met his gaze. "Why does it matter, Ben? Why is everyone so interested?"

Ben sighed, glancing away, "Because, Sienna, Dylan's a Whitmore. There are expectations, stories, history..."

"You know we care about you." Maya intervened. "We just don't want to see you hurt."

The raw wound of their hike together throbbed in Sienna's consciousness. It jarred that, aside from today, she had not seen Dylan at all. They'd made plans, which he canceled, a fact she'd concealed from even Maya. That slight felt personal, and she harbored the sting, tucking it away behind a facade of indifference even as it gnawed at her.

"The Whitmore family is...complicated," Maya remarked.

Sienna smiled. "Aren't all families?"

Maya and Ben exchanged glances, the unspoken agreement to drop the topic clear between them. The trio continued with lighter banter for a while longer, but Sienna's thoughts kept drifting back to Dylan.

After her friends had left, Sienna pulled out her phone, her fingers hovering over the screen before she typed out a message: "Hey Dylan, hope all's well. Will I see you again?"

She hit send and the familiar anxiety of waiting for a reply settled in her stomach. Minutes passed, feeling more like hours, and then she saw it—the read receipt. But those minutes turned into more minutes, and no reply came. The uncertainty gnawed at her.

Sienna felt the urge to drown her unease with some distraction. Instead of heading straight to her room, she detoured to the resort's business center, eager to delve deeper into the legend of Eliza Goodwin.

Once engrossed in her research, hours slipped away, and by the time she left the business center, the resort was blanketed in the cool embrace of night. Sienna chose the scenic route back, hoping the beauty of the gardens under the moonlit sky would clear her head.

At night, the gardens transformed into a serene, almost otherworldly space. Moonlight streamed through the branches, casting silvery pools of light along the pathways while crickets chirped a soothing nocturnal melody. For a moment, Sienna felt a sense of peace, the stresses of the day melting away.

But as she continued, the shadows lengthened, and the air grew chillier. An eerie feeling crept up her spine, giving her the unsettling impression that she was being watched. Her heart beat faster, and she picked up her pace. When she glanced over her shoulder—nothing but the deepening darkness met her eyes.

She hurried back to the building that housed her room. As she turned the corner to her hallway, she saw a familiar silhouette leaning against the door to her room.

Dylan.

He looked up as she approached, his blue eyes intense in the dim light. Without a word, he stepped forward, bridging the gap between them. She took a step back.

He raised his hands in a gesture of peace. "I didn't mean to startle you."

After taking the time to gather herself, she managed a weak smile. "It's okay. Just been one of those days." She motioned for him to follow her inside. But as the door opened wider, the animated chatter of her roommates ceased. Three sets of eyes darting between Sienna and the handsome figure behind her. The weight of their stares was palpable.

Dylan cleared his throat, breaking the tense silence. "Maybe we could go somewhere else?"

She hesitated for just a moment, then agreed, and they made their way to the parking lot. The roar of the engine from Dylan's sleek BMW coupe seemed to symbolize the vast difference in their worlds. As they drove away from the resorts grounds, Sienna glanced at Dylan's profile, noticing the tension in his jaw and the worry lines that seemed more pronounced tonight.

Finally, he broke the silence.

"I'm sorry," Dylan began, his eyes still fixed on the road but his tone sincere. "For earlier. I saw you, and I just... I couldn't help myself."

Sienna's gaze shifted from the window to him. She was torn between anger and desire. "You ignore my texts, vanish without explanation, and then think you can just pull me into a corner to make out?" Her voice trembled.

Dylan sighed, running a hand through his hair. "I know. It's complicated, Sienna."

She turned to face him, her frustration clear. "Isn't everything with you? One minute you're the charming guy who swept me off my feet on our hike, and the next, you're distant and elusive, always hiding behind vague excuses."

He pulled into an overlook and turned off the engine. Then he faced her, taking a deep breath. "Sienna, you have every right to be angry. And I promise I'll explain everything.... But none of that excuses how I've been acting. You deserve better."

Sienna took a moment, trying to calm the storm inside her. "Dylan, I'm not some plaything you can pick up and drop when you feel like it. I thought we had something real, something special. But now, I just feel like I'm caught in this whirlwind that is Dylan Whitmore, and I don't know how to find my footing."

He reached out, taking her hand.

Sienna took a deep breath. "Look, Dylan, I can handle whispers and sidelong glances. But I need you to be honest with me. What's really going on?"

Dylan turned away for a moment, collecting himself. "My stepmom... she's been very sick. It's been hard on all of us." He admitted, his voice quivering.

Sienna's gaze softened. "I've heard the rumors. They talk at the resort, you know?"

He nodded. "I figured as much. What they don't know is that she's been more than just a stepmother to me. My mom passed away when I was just a baby. She stepped in, raising me as her own. We're close, incredibly close. And watching her suffer… it's tearing me apart."

Sienna reached out, placing a comforting hand on his. "I'm sorry, Dylan. I did not know."

He smiled, "Thank you. And on top of all that, the family dynamics… they're not normal… it's all a bit much."

She raised an eyebrow.

Dylan hesitated, his voice lowering. "There's something else," he sighed. "Remember the old woman at the diner? She mentioned Eliza's curse. My family avoids the topic, but whispers of it linger—they all believe in it. It's like an old family legend, the curse of the Whitmores."

A chill ran down Sienna's spine. "The same curse?" she asked.

He nodded. "Actually, the real reason I was on that hike the day we met was to see if connecting with Eliza might help my mom get better. But I found nothing."

"Nothing?" Sienna arched an eyebrow, her curiosity piqued. "I'm not so sure about that."

Dylan cracked a smile, and he brushed her cheek. "There was you, and you're definitely not nothing."

Sienna leaned in, her face flushing. "I've been looking into Eliza Goodwin's legend. The story has… captivated me," she confessed.

"It's a big part of our family history," Dylan acknowledged. "A tragic story of love, betrayal, and heartbreak. But the curse—it's believed to bring misfortune to any Whitmore who falls in love. Most the men in our family choose not to fall in love. My father was different- he did it twice."

Sienna, piecing everything together, suddenly realized the complexity of their relationship. Dylan's hesitance wasn't just about his stepmother's illness or his responsibilities at the resort. He was grappling with the fear of a curse, worried about what their growing closeness could mean for both of them.

Dylan let out a long breath. "It sounds crazy, right? But when I think about my family's past, I can't help but wonder. I've tried to talk about it with my dad and grandfather, but they shut it down quickly. My grandfather just warns, 'Don't fall in love,' and my dad... he doesn't want to believe it's real. To them, it's just a tale, but I've experienced things, felt things that make me think there's more to it."

Dylan paused, his gaze shifting to the dark road beyond the windshield. He swallowed hard, his Adam's apple bobbing. "There's something else I haven't shared, something I should have."

Sienna placed a comforting hand on his arm. "You can tell me, Dylan."

He took a deep breath, the grip on the steering wheel tightening before he relaxed. "Ever since that day in the woods, I haven't been sleeping well. At first, I thought it was just the stress of everything with my family. But then... every time I close my eyes, I see you."

Sienna's heart raced at his words, unsure of where he was going with this. She remained silent.

"In my dreams, it's always you," he continued, his voice shaky. "At first, it's beautiful—scenes of us laughing, walking together, or sharing moments. But then, they take a dark turn. I see all these terrible things happening to you—accidents, dangers, shadows closing in. I can't explain it, but it feels so real, as if they're premonitions."

Sienna's breath caught. "Premonitions?"

Dylan shook his head, frustration clear. "I don't know. It feels different, more vivid than regular nightmares. And the worst part is, I'm helpless in those dreams. I try reaching out to you, but something always stops me. It's like a constant reminder of the Whitmore curse, and I can't shake the feeling that by bringing you closer to me, I'm putting you in harm's way."

Sienna processed his words. She thought of her own experiences, the whispers she heard, the mysterious encounters at the resort. But looking at Dylan, the raw vulnerability in his eyes, she felt a rush of protectiveness.

"I've felt something too since our hike." Sienna's voice was gentle. "Whispers when no one's around, cold gusts on warm nights. I didn't want to believe, but after what's been happening..."

They shared a moment, both lost in the legends and the strange events surrounding them.

Dylan broke the silence, "Being with you this summer, it's been unexpected, and it feels different from anything I've known. But with these rumors, the family tales, and now your experiences... it scares me."

Sienna paused, keeping her gaze fixed on Dylan. "Dylan, these legends... they're stories. They are echoes of the past. We're here, in the present. And while I respect them, we can't let them overshadow us." She reached out, touching his hand. "Whatever we face, we face together."

His eyes met hers. "Thank you, Sienna. That means more than you know."

They sat in silence, enveloped by the night's stillness at the overlook—only the distant chirping of crickets and the occasional rustle of leaves breaking the quiet. Above, the stars twinkled, their soft, silvery light filtering through the car's sunroof.

Sienna turned to Dylan. "You know, it's weird," she whispered, "everything about this place, this moment... it feels like it's out of time."

He smiled, tucking a stray lock of her hair behind her ear. "Feels like the universe just paused everything for us, doesn't it? Just to let us be here, together."

They drifted from casual childhood stories to more revealing conversations. As they delved deeper, the space between them seemed to close, leaving them in a comfort of shared truths and raw emotion.

After another bout of quiet, Dylan took a deep breath and asked, "About all the ghost stories... Can you tell me more?"

She was relieved to share her concerns. "It's been really bizarre. I keep waking up to what sounds like lullabies. I see shadows flickering just beyond direct sight, and there's this weird chill that seems to linger around me."

Dylan's expression grew serious. "Eliza's history isn't just a tale. I can't shake the feeling that she's at the heart of the curse."

"You really think it's all real? Eliza and the curse?" Sienna asked.

He nodded. "I have a plan, a way we might figure this out. Are you free Monday?"

Sienna hesitated, memories of past disappointments clouding her expression. "Dylan, just promise me you won't bail this time."

"I can't change the past," Dylan said, his voice firm. "But I promise, this time I'll be there. No more letdowns."

Sienna paused, considering. Finally, she nodded. "Alright, I trust you. Monday it is."

Their moment was shattered by the ring of Dylan's phone. His hand tightened around hers before he pulled away. As he answered, his casual confidence shifted to concern.

"It's my stepmom," he murmured, anxiety threading through his voice as he tried to stay composed. "They've taken her to the hospital. I have to go."

Sienna felt a pang of sympathy for him. The vulnerability that had enveloped them earlier was now overshadowed by the urgent reality crashing in.

"I'm so sorry," she whispered.

He nodded, his face tense as he fought to maintain control. "Thanks. It's just... it's been tough, watching her fade and feeling so helpless."

They sat together for a minute before Dylan started the car, breaking the silence with its steady hum. The drive back to the resort was quiet, each lost in their thoughts. When they arrived, he parked and turned to her, his face lined with strain.

"I'm sorry our evening ended like this," he breathed.

She leaned in and kissed him. "It's okay. Life throws us curveballs. Just focus on your family right now. And when you're ready, I'll be here."

With one last look, he stepped out of the car and watched her walk into the resort. The night had been a rollercoaster of emotions, but as Sienna lay in bed later, one thing was clear: her bond with Dylan was just beginning, and whatever challenges lay ahead, they would face them together.

CHAPTER SIX

Gifts of the Heart

Sienna had grown accustomed to the familiar hum of the White Pine Resort staff lounge, a refuge from her duties, always alive with chatter and camaraderie. Yet, something had shifted this evening.

Golden light washed over the patterned carpets lining the hallways, its warm glow stark against the cool undercurrents of tension Sienna felt as she approached the employee lounge. Words, snippets of hushed conversations, reached her ears and halted abruptly as she reached the threshold.

"... Dylan and her, alone at the—"

"...you'd think she'd have more sense, getting involved with—"

"... the Whitmore name and a mere—"

Each broken fragment pricked at her consciousness like a thorn. Sienna took a deep breath and entered. The room, with its melange of overstuffed chairs and dark woods bathed in soft ambient lighting, seemed to pause. A few heads turned, eyes meeting hers briefly before darting away. Conversations that had been lively seconds ago fell mute, replaced by artificial smiles and furtive glances among her colleagues.

She tried to dispel the unease, reminding herself she had done nothing wrong. Her relationship with Dylan was unexpected, but undeniably genuine. Yet, each step she took intensified the gnawing sensation in her stomach, like tendrils of smoke curling around her insides, planting seeds of doubt.

Was their connection fodder for every whispered rumor? Had their private moments turned into a public spectacle? Each shadowy glance and unspoken insinuation deepened her sense of violation.

She attempted to maintain her routine, exchanging casual pleasantries and making sure not to linger in one place too long. But even as she immersed herself in tasks, the undercurrents of gossip persisted. A colleague brushed past her, releasing an almost imperceptible sigh. Their fingers grazed, and the woman whispered, "Be careful, love. Not everyone wishes you well."

Sienna paused, stunned. The boundary between her professional life and personal feelings for Dylan blurred. How had something so pure become so corrupted in the mouths of others?

As the evening progressed, Sienna felt like an outsider. The resort seemed a labyrinth of mirrors, each reflection distorting her image. The real Sienna, the one who laughed and loved, seemed lost amid these warped perceptions.

She leaned against the balcony railing and took a deep breath of the night air. The complexity of her relationship with Dylan made her question the depth and authenticity of their connection. What was real, and how much had been tainted by the judgments of others?

The soft rustle of leaves and distant chatter from below provided a backdrop to her contemplation. But it was the quiet approach of footsteps that drew her out of her thoughts. Turning, she saw Dylan, the usual spark in his eyes replaced with weariness. However, his presence, even during uncertainty, was comforting, grounding her amidst the chaos.

Without a word, he stepped closer, enveloping her in his embrace. The world seemed to shrink, their shared heartbeats the only sound that mattered. She felt the slight tremble in his frame and tightened her grip, wanting to offer whatever solace she could.

"She's stable," Dylan whispered, his voice carrying a mix of relief and exhaustion. "They're letting her come home tomorrow."

Sienna could feel the emotion behind his words. "Tell me about her," she prompted.

Dylan leaned back against the railing, looking out into the night. "She's been everything to me. My mom passed when I was a baby, but when my dad remarried, my stepmother stepped in and never made me feel any less loved. She's kind, generous..."

He paused, the pain clear in his down-turned eyes. "My father, he's never been the same since he lost my mom. Something inside him broke. And he doesn't always treat my stepmother the way she deserves. It's complicated. My grandmother also passed away young, so she's the only consistent female figure I've had."

Tears welled in Sienna's eyes, spurred by the pain of Dylan's revelations and the relief of his stepmother's recovery. She reached out, cradling his face in her hands. "Dylan, that's wonderful news about her coming home." Overcome with emotion, she pressed her lips to his in a deep, comforting kiss.

Time seemed to stand still as they savored the moment. Yet their bubble of intimacy was shattered by a flicker at the edge of Sienna's vision. They pulled apart and turned towards the shadows at the balcony's fringe. There, caught in the interplay of moonlight and darkness, was a fleeting movement—too swift to decipher. Was it merely the echoes of the Whitmore curse or someone with intentions far more tangible?

Sienna's heart raced, her hand reaching for Dylan's. "Did you see that?" she whispered.

He nodded, scanning the area. "I did."

Silence surrounded them once more. Dylan squeezed Sienna's hand. "I should go," he murmured.

She nodded, understanding his need to be with his family and away from the prying eyes that seemed to be everywhere. "Be safe, Dylan," she said.

He smiled, pressing a soft kiss to her forehead. "Always."

With that, he disappeared into the night, leaving Sienna with a growing sense of unease. Whether they were being watched by someone from this realm or another, the challenges they faced were only growing.

Sienna's footsteps echoed on the polished floors of the resort as she clocked out, the residual stress of her shift dissipating. The familiar sight of Maya waiting by the lockers brought a much-needed smile to her face.

"Finally!" Maya exclaimed, looping her arm around Sienna's. "I was thinking we'd need a search party! How about the cafe?"

Sienna nodded, grateful for Maya's attempt to keep things light. Together, they made their way through the resort's corridors to the cafe next to the main lounge.

As Sienna sipped her latte and Maya chatted animatedly, the peace was shattered by Lila and Monica's abrupt arrival. Their confidence was palpable, and their intrusion was no accident.

"We saw you two from across the room and just had to join," Monica said, her tone veiling her true intentions. Without waiting for an invitation, both women slid into the booth beside them.

Lila's gaze swept over Sienna, her lips twisting into a smirk. "Spending a lot of time with Dylan, I hear. Reminds me of last summer when he couldn't look away from me."

Monica's laugh rang hollow. "Those Whitmore men—always on to the next best thing."

Maya rolled her eyes. "What do you want? If you're here to stir up old stories, find another table."

Lila ignored Maya and leaned closer. "Just thought you should know what you're getting into with Dylan. His little... adventures never last."

Monica's smirk widened. "Be careful, dear. You wouldn't want to be just another Whitmore conquest."

Though Maya tensed, ready to confront them, Sienna took a deep breath and responded with composure, "Thank you for the advice, but my relationship with Dylan is none of your business."

As the duo left with a final smug glance, Maya exhaled. "Why must they meddle in everything?"

Sienna's lips curled into a mischievous smile, her fingers tracing the rim of her coffee mug. "You know, Maya, Dylan and I... we kissed. And it was magical."

Maya's eyes lit up, her initial surprise turning into a beaming smile. "Really? Oh, Si! That's wonderful!"

But as her excitement surged, her protective side emerged. "I'm thrilled for you, Sienna. Just promise me you'll be careful? I want the best for you, especially in love."

Sienna met Maya's earnest gaze. "I promise, Maya. And thank you for always having my back."

Whispers, insinuations, and sidelong glances had spun a story in Sienna's mind she hadn't considered before. What had Dylan done to earn such a notorious reputation? Doubts loomed large, yet amid the voices in her head, reason prevailed. It reminded her of the toxic nature of gossip and how easily distorted stories could skew perception. Sienna resolved to find the truth from Dylan.

Sienna replayed Lila's and Monica's veiled warnings and overt insinuations. Determined to understand the truth from Dylan himself, she pulled out her phone and sent him a message. His almost immediate reply told her he was in the offices.

Despite the possibility of waiting for a more appropriate moment, the urgency to confront him propelled her forward. She approached one of the resort's grand halls, reserved for formal events. The unmistakable deep resonance of Dylan's voice reached her ears, piquing her curiosity.

Sienna tucked herself behind an ornate marble pillar and listened. The familiar, authoritative tones of Dylan's father and grandfather carried through their hushed but intense conversation, sending a thrill of urgency through her veins.

"Understand, Dylan," his father's voice was authoritative, "the Whitmore reputation is paramount. It's not just about us, it's generations of hard work and legacy. We can't afford another scandal."

Dylan's voice carried a note of frustration. "I understand, Dad. But what does that have to do with—"

"The last one," his grandfather cut in, his voice dripping with disdain. "Remember? How we had to clean up after? We won't let that happen again."

Sienna's heart sank, her mind racing. What were they talking about? What "last one"?

"I know what happened," Dylan responded, tension clear in his tone. "But Sienna is different—"

"Like the others said they were?" his father countered, his voice dripping with sarcasm. "Or have you forgotten so quickly?"

The room went silent for a moment, the tension palpable. "Alright," Dylan conceded, his voice a whisper. "I'll end it. I'll do what's best for the family."

Sienna's heart felt like it was being squeezed in a vise. She'd expected Dylan to stand up for her, to counter his family's apparent disapproval. But he seemed to fold under their pressure, leaving her feeling betrayed.

Tears pricked Sienna's eyes as she backed away. Had Dylan discussed their private moments with his family? Or was she being judged based on unknown past events? The weight of her insecurities, compounded by the sting of perceived betrayal, made it hard to breathe.

She needed space to think. Sienna vowed to uncover the truth, but the glimpse into a world she wasn't prepared for left her reeling.

The fading echoes of Dylan's conversation with his father and grandfather reverberated in the hallway. Pressed against the cold wall, hidden by a tapestry depicting some historic event, Sienna felt the oppressive weight of the overheard words. Each heartbeat seemed to echo the painful revelations.

She risked a glance around the corner and caught Dylan's eye. His usually confident gaze was now clouded with desperation. He stepped towards her, his mouth parting as if to speak, but Sienna, driven by instinct, turned and fled.

As she hurried out, Dylan attempted to follow, but was obstructed by his imposing grandfather.

"Dylan!" the elder Whitmore's voice boomed. "Where do you think you're going?"

Twilight cast a silvery glow over the sprawling estate as Sienna's steps quickened, each one in sync with the frantic beating of her heart. Dylan's voice echoed behind her.

"Sienna! Wait!"

His tone carried a raw edge of pain. Yet, driven by a tumult of betrayal, shock, and pain, Sienna increased her pace, desperate to distance herself from Dylan and the confining legacy of the Whitmore family.

She didn't look back. With every fiber urging her on, she sprinted through the gardens, past the blurred faces of staff and guests, towards the sanctuary of the staff quarters.

Once safe, she darted to her workstation. Settling in, a suffocating weight descended upon her chest. Every corner of the space, filled with memories of her moments with Dylan, seemed to echo a haunting web of deception.

She needed a break from this place.

As she approached her supervisor, she blurted, "I need some time off," her voice strained. "A family emergency."

The woman raised an eyebrow. But seeing the raw pain in Sienna's eyes, nodded in understanding. "Very well. But not for too long. We're nearing peak season."

With a brisk nod, Sienna rushed back to her quarters. She started gathering essentials: a hiking backpack, a small tent, and enough food for a few days. As she moved about, the familiar process of preparing for a solo hike brought calm. The repetitive act of rolling, folding, and packing grounded her amidst the emotional storm she found herself in.

However, as she zipped up her backpack, a sudden chill swept the room. The soft, unmistakable whisper of a ghostly voice sent shivers down her spine, its message clear, "Good. Get far away from here." The voice seemed to emanate from the very walls, wrapping around her like a spectral embrace. It was as if the spirits of White Pines were urging her onward, pushing her away from the looming danger and heartbreak.

Maya's face flashed in her mind, but she hesitated, deciding against telling her. She couldn't bear another conversation, another round of advice or sympathy.

The shroud of night had already cloaked the Frozen Tears trailhead by the time Sienna arrived. Darkness engulfed her, the dense canopy above smothering the few stubborn stars trying to pierce through. She clicked her headlamp to life, its pale beam cutting a path through the gloom, stretching shadows into eerie figures that mimicked her ascent.

The path was both familiar and alien, transformed under the nocturnal veil. Daytime sounds lay subdued, while the night amplified whispers of the wilderness: leaves fluttering in a breeze, an owl's distant lament, the ceaseless dirge of crickets and frogs.

She was drawn toward the cave that had protected her and Dylan from the rain. As she got closer, the burdens of Dylan's mysteries and her own chaotic emotions lifted, muted by the forest's age-old whispers. The cave's entrance loomed, resembling the gaping maw of a benevolent giant, offering her a strange solace in its dark embrace.

A cold blast greeted Sienna as she neared, forcing her to wrap her sweatshirt tighter. The cave's chill contradicted the balmy evening, sending shivers through her as if warning her of the foreboding within.

She stepped inside and the light from her headlamp flickered across the damp walls, casting unsettling shadows. As she settled into the cave's embrace, a tension thickened the air, intensifying the unease that clung to her like a second skin.

A soft whisper floated towards her, like the gentle hum of a distant song. She halted, trying to discern the source, but the sound vanished as quickly as it came. A quiet giggle echoed in the confines of the cave, a girlish laugh tinged with a shade of melancholy.

"Hello?" Sienna called out, her voice trembling. The giggle intensified, transforming into a series of heart-wrenching sobs. An icy chill enveloped her, and she felt an unseen presence, its pain palpable, its sorrow tangible.

With a bravery she didn't know she had, Sienna whispered, "Eliza?"

The noise ceased, replaced by silence. Then, as if summoned from the very walls of the cave, a figure materialized before Sienna's eyes. The ghostly apparition of a young woman stood before her, dressed in period clothing, her eyes sorrowful yet intense.

"Eliza," Sienna whispered again, a strange connection drawing her to the spirit.

The ghostly figure nodded. "Betrayed by love, betrayed by trust. He took all, left me in the dust."

Sienna's heart ached for the lost soul before her. "I'm here, Eliza. I'm listening," she whispered.

A single tear slid down Eliza's cheek. "John, he promised forever, but his words were but lies. Left with the Colonel, chasing false skies."

Sienna, thinking of her own heartbreak with Dylan, felt a deep kinship with the spirit. "I know what betrayal feels like," she murmured, reaching out a hand towards Eliza.

The temperature in the cave seemed to drop an oppressive cold emanating from the ethereal form of Eliza. Her sorrowful eyes darkened with rage, her voice taking on a sharp, chilling edge. "The Whitmores have taken much from me. They've sown seeds of deception, and now they shall reap what they've sown."

Sienna took a step back, sensing the shift in Eliza's energy. The spectral figure continued, her voice dripping with malice, "They think they can continue their games. That time would have dulled my vengeance. But every Whitmore who betrays will know my wrath."

Sienna's heart raced. The thought of Dylan in danger took precedence over every other emotion. "Eliza, please," she pleaded with urgency, her voice thick with apprehension, "don't harm Dylan. Regardless of his family's past actions, he should not be the one to endure your anger."

A wicked smile curled the edges of Eliza's lips. "We shall see," she hissed, her eyes glinting with a malevolent light.

The form dissipated, and the cave grew darker. Sienna's heart pounded in her chest. The threat felt imminent. Time seemed to stand still as she fumbled with her phone, tried to find a signal to call or warn Dylan. Panic set in when she realized she was cut off from the outside world.

The night air seemed to press against her as Sienna scrambled through the dense woods. Every rustle seemed amplified. The path she once found serene now felt ominous. In her haste, she stumbled over an exposed tree root, her knee slamming into the hard ground. Pain shot through her, but she pushed herself up, her need to warn Dylan fueling her movements.

She made it to the parking lot, her chest heaving. Her hand shook as she retrieved her phone, dialing Dylan's number. He answered almost immediately, but his voice sounded strained, sending a fresh wave of anxiety through her.

Panic surged through Sienna's veins as she heard Dylan's voice on the other end, strained but alive. "Sienna, I'm okay," he began, his breaths coming out ragged. "There was this woman, standing right in the middle of the road. I had no time, and I just... I swerved. The next thing I knew, the car was spinning out of control. I could feel the drop just inches away. It's a miracle I didn't go over."

Sienna pressed a hand to her chest, feeling her heart hammering against her ribcage. The haunting words of Eliza echoed in her mind. "Oh my God, Dylan! You could have been..." She couldn't even finish the thought.

He continued, "The car's in bad shape, maybe totaled. But by some luck, I escaped with just some scrapes." There was a pause, and when he spoke again, his voice held a hint of vulnerability. "Sienna, it was close."

The swell of emotions threatening to overwhelm her as she responded, "Where are you? Just tell me. I'll come get you. We'll figure everything out together."

After Dylan relayed his location, Sienna sped in that direction. Upon finding him, she slowed the car to a stop, and he got in. The quiet hum of the engine filled the space between them as Sienna then pulled over to a more secluded spot under the wash of orange streetlights. The dim light inside the car cast long shadows, accentuating the raw emotions flickering across their faces.

Dylan's fingers trembled as he undid his seatbelt, turning to face Sienna. In a moment of mutual need, they reached for each other, their embrace serving as an anchor amidst the emotional storm swirling around them. The warmth they shared spoke volumes, offering silent comfort and reassurance.

Still reeling from her intense encounter in the cave, Sienna felt an urgent need to share everything. As she recounted her brush with the spectral Eliza Goodwin, Dylan's face, already pale, blanched further. Her story seemed to mirror the threats and challenges that had been haunting their relationship from the start.

Dylan ran his hands through his disheveled hair. "Sienna," he began, his voice hoarse, "I've been meaning to tell you something, to clear the air between us. But I never knew how."

Her eyes urged him to continue.

"That girl," he started, "the one everyone talks about? We had a few dates, nothing serious. But then she came to me with the pregnancy claim. I was shocked." His eyes held a mix of anger and vulnerability. "It couldn't have been mine. We never... we never did that.."

He looked away, lost in the memories of that tumultuous period. "But it was her word against mine. My family, with their obsession with our image, took matters into their hands. They believed paying her off was the best way to protect both me and the Whitmore name."

Sienna felt a wave of empathy wash over her. The burden of carrying an ancient family name, with its limitless expectations and relentless scrutiny, was something she could only imagine.

Dylan met her gaze once more, his eyes searching hers for understanding. "It's not just the scandal. There have been too many people who've gotten close to me with ulterior motives, looking to capitalize on the Whitmore legacy. My family wanted to protect me. But in doing so, they ended up isolating me behind walls."

Sienna absorbed his words, her thoughts racing. She recalled Eliza's warnings—the vengeful spirit determined to haunt the Whitmores. Was it all connected? The past and present tangled in a complex web of love, betrayal, and secrets?

Turning to face Dylan, she searched his eyes for sincerity. "We're both being tested in different ways. But if we stand together, if we stay honest with each other, we can overcome this."

Dylan nodded, squeezing her hand. "I want that. More than anything." He rubbed the back of his neck and added, "I really don't want to go home right now. Could you drop me off at a motel or something?"

Sienna nodded in understanding, feeling his need for distance from the White Pines Resort. "Of course, Dylan. I know a quiet place not too far from here."

He looked at her, vulnerability in his eyes. "Would you… stay with me? Just for the night? I could use the company."

Sienna, recognizing the genuine plea in his voice, replied, "Of course."

The dim light from a neon "Vacancy" sign led them to a modest motel, with rows of doors opening to the parking lot. The surrounding area was quiet, with only the faint chirp of crickets breaking the stillness. Dylan glanced at Sienna, a wordless question in his eyes. She nodded, and they made their way to the front office.

They registered under Sienna's name for discretion and out of an unspoken agreement that, for now, they needed to keep things as low-key as possible.

The motel room was a stark contrast to the opulent halls of the Whitmore resort. A faded floral bedspread covered the queen-sized bed, matched by patterned curtains. The carpet, showing signs of wear, had seen better days. A small television perched on a dresser, its blank screen mirroring back at them. The air held a faint mix of old cigarette smoke and cleaning agents.

For Sienna, the room was familiar. It was reminiscent of the countless nights she'd spent in such places during her childhood travels with her parents. They couldn't afford fancy hotels, so these budget motels had been their tempo-rary havens. Memories flooded back—her parents' whispered conversations late at night, the comforting touch of threadbare motel blankets, and the thrill of exploring a new place, even if it was just another nondescript motel.

She glanced at Dylan, curious about his reaction to the room. There was no hint of disdain or discomfort on his face. Instead, he surveyed the room with a quiet curiosity, as if exploring a chapter of life he had never known.

After settling in, the day's burdens seemed to weigh heavier on them. Dylan broke the silence first. "You know, there's something comforting about this place. It's simple, without pretense. It's just... real."

Sienna smiled, touched by his insight. "It's quite a shift from what you're used to."

He nodded, "It is. But right now, there's nowhere else I'd rather be."

The room's lone lamp cast a soft amber glow, illuminating the inviting bed. Its worn sheets, though far from luxurious, promised a comfort that the pristine beds of White Pines could never offer.

Dylan glanced at the couch, then back at Sienna. "I can take the couch tonight, if you'd prefer the bed to yourself," he offered.

Sienna smiled, touched by his consideration. "I don't mind sharing. Just to sleep, though."

Dylan nodded, understanding her need for closeness without crossing boundaries. He turned down the covers, gesturing for Sienna to climb in first. She hesitated for a moment, appreciating his respect for her space, then slid under the sheets. Dylan joined her, settling into the mattress at a respectful distance.

They lay side by side, their fingers interlocking in a gesture of silent understanding and support. Sienna turned to face him, her expression soft. "It's been a long day," she murmured.

"Yes, but it's better now," Dylan replied, his voice low and reassuring.

As they talked about their experiences and the mysteries they were unraveling, their connection felt more genuine. Their conversation tapered off into a comfortable silence. Surrounded by the simple peace of the room, the day's tensions dissolved and Sienna drifted off to sleep.

CHAPTER SEVEN

Echos of the Past

Sienna awoke to the comforting aroma of coffee. Her eyelids fluttered open, and memories of the previous night flooded back. Dylan stood there with a gentle smile, offering a steaming cup. "Thought you might like this," he murmured.

The simple gesture warmed her heart. The coffee, likely from the motel lobby, felt like the most thoughtful gift in that moment. "Thank you," she whispered.

As they sipped their coffee, the warm liquid mingling with the soft glow inside them, Dylan broke the silence. "Remember, I planned a day for us. Seems even more fitting now." His soft baritone carried a hint of mystery, piquing her curiosity.

"What are we doing?" she asked, her eyes alight with anticipation.

He shook his head. "It's a surprise."

With a chuckle, Sienna let the mystery engulf her, basking in the joy it brought. They set off, her car humming as Dylan guided it along winding roads. Outside, the landscape was a tapestry of nature's rich hues, where greens and blues merged in a dance that seemed to whisper ancient secrets of earth and sky.

The car came to a halt in front of a white building adorned with grand pillars, a beacon of knowledge in the quaint town of Bartlett, NH. Sienna's heart fluttered with confusion as she gazed at the public library. "A library?" she murmured, puzzled.

They stepped inside and were greeted by the scents of aged paper and bound leather, each carrying tales of old, eager to be discovered. A gentleman with a warm, welcoming demeanor stood waiting, an open book in his hand.

The library's intimate space radiated a hushed reverence, its corners alive with the echoes of ancient stories and past readers. Drawn by curiosity, Sienna's steps were tentative as she followed Dylan toward the back of the room, where a tall, lean figure awaited among the shelves.

Mr. Richardson, a silver-haired man with spectacles resting on his hawkish nose, looked up as they approached.

His sharp, discerning eyes met Sienna's, their intensity catching her off guard.

"Dylan," Mr. Richardson greeted, nodding at the younger man before turning his piercing gaze back to Sienna. "And you must be Sienna. A pleasure to meet you."

Sienna smiled, trying to quell the trepidation rising within her. "Mr. Richardson," she replied. "Thank you for seeing us."

The elderly archivist smiled, a soft, reassuring expression that put Sienna at ease. "Ah, my dear, when Dylan contacted me regarding your interest in the history of Eliza Goodwin, I couldn't resist. Our town's history is full of fascinating tales, and that of Eliza and the Whitmores are among its most poignant."

Dylan squeezed Sienna's hand, guiding her to a large oak table laden with materials. There were yellowed letters tied in faded ribbons, paintings whose colors had withstood the test of time, and newspaper clippings that told tales of love, betrayal, and mystery.

Sienna's fingers traced the words on the page, feeling the textured grooves of the dried ink, each stroke heavy with emotion. The letter revealed a heart full of longing, a soul grappling with forbidden desires and societal constraints. Each note, signed with Eliza's distinct flourish, was a declaration of a love that transcended time and boundaries.

Beside the letters there lay a series of detailed sketches. One sketch depicted Eliza, her hair flowing down her back, her eyes a complex mix of sorrow and hope. Next to her stood a man, John, his posture protective, his eyes filled with love and resolve.

As Sienna studied Eliza's portrait, a realization dawned on her. The resemblance was striking; this was the same figure that had appeared before her, the same face that had haunted her dreams and materialized on the road. A shiver traveled down her spine.

Dylan leaned in, his voice a whisper. "That's her, Sienna. The woman I almost hit on the road."

What gripped Sienna's attention were the aged newspaper clippings. Yellowed with time, they whispered tales of the notorious Whitmore curse. They detailed heart-wrenching stories of those who defied it, their lives cut short, leaving behind dreams that never saw the light of day.

As Sienna absorbed each word, a weight seemed to settle deeper within her. The tragic romance of Eliza and John mirrored her growing feelings for Dylan, stirring a chilling thought: Was history doomed to repeat itself?

Mr. Richardson, observing her concern, said, "The past is filled with stories, some unsettling. But remember, history records what was, not what must be. You and Dylan shape your own futures."

The atmosphere in the library thickened when Mr. Richardson presented a detailed genealogical chart. Its delicate branches of family connections sprawled like a web, each name and date meticulously noted. He unrolled it, exposing the intricate network of lives intertwined.

"There's something you should see, Miss Avery," he murmured, directing Sienna's gaze to a specific branch of the chart. Her eyes traced from Eliza Goodwin's name to her sister's, spanning generations, until landing on a familiar name—Sienna Avery.

Her breath caught, a mix of awe and shock. "This... this means I'm descended from Eliza Goodwin's family?"

Mr. Richardson nodded with understanding. "Yes, through her sister."

Sienna turned to Dylan, emotions swirling. "How did you find this?"

Dylan looked away, his expression tinged with sheepishness. "I had help from HR. I wanted to understand more about our history, our connection."

Dylan's access hinted at resources beyond mere wealth, suggesting he might use the resort's HR department to delve into her past. The potential power dynamics were unsettling, as she considered the implications of his actions.

Mr. Richardson then introduced another item—a box bearing the Avery family crest. Inside, a worn, leather-bound journal with 'Avery' embossed in faded gold caught her attention. As Sienna flipped through its pages, recounting interactions with the Whitmores across centuries, the weight of their shared history settled in.

She looked up to meet Dylan's gaze, and a question hung in the air: How much did he know about her life now?

A soft chime from Dylan's wristwatch cut through the tension. He checked it, then met her eyes with a grave look. "We have one more appointment to make, Sienna."

Mr. Richardson began gathering the historical artifacts, placing them back into their respective boxes. "It's been a pleasure sharing this history with both of you," he commented, handing Sienna his card. "Should you have any more questions, don't hesitate to reach out."

Sienna clasped the card, her voice warm with gratitude. "Thank you, Mr. Richardson. I never realized how deeply our lives are intertwined with the threads of the past."

Outside, the sun streamed down. As Sienna and Dylan made their way to her Toyota, she could feel a myriad of emotions swirling within her — a mix of shock, fascination, and anticipation.

As she settled into the driver's seat, Dylan turned to her, taking a deep breath. "Before we go any further, I thought I'd tell you where we're heading next. It's a bit... unconventional, but I remembered how you said the paranormal intrigued you."

Sienna's eyes went wide, her heartbeat kicking up a notch. "Go on," she encouraged, leaning forward.

He paused, his eyes locked on hers. "We're meeting a psychic medium who deals with ghosts of unrequited love and star-crossed lovers. Given everything we've dug up today, it seems like the perfect fit. Her name's Ashlyn."

"Ashlyn Alden? The psychic from that ghost hunter show?"

A grin spread across Dylan's face. "Yeah, that's her. I figured someone with her clout could really shed some light on things."

Excitement surged through Sienna. "No way, I've seen all her episodes! She's unreal! This is gonna be epic, Dylan." She paused, catching her breath, her mind racing with the possibilities of what they might discover with Ashlyn.

She started the car and said, "Alright, lead the way. Let's find out what the spirits are dying to tell us."

The car slid into a parking spot of another grand resort, different from the Whitmore estate, yet equally opulent. As Dylan adjusted the rearview mirror, he reached into his backpack and pulled out a baseball cap, placing it on his head. A playful smirk danced on his lips.

"Don't want the competition spotting a Whitmore dining in their territory," he joked, winking at Sienna.

Sienna chuckled, shaking her head. "Your secret's safe with me," she teased.

They approached the resort's pub, named "The Tap House." It had a rustic charm to it, with dark wooden beams and low lighting. Before they even entered, Sienna felt the charged atmosphere that seemed to hint at both history and mystery.

The door chime announced their entrance, and almost immediately, Sienna's gaze was drawn to a table near the window. There, bathed in the gentle glow of the afternoon sun, sat a woman who could only be described as enchanting.

Ashlyn Alden had an aura of mystique about her that was undeniable. Even without the captivating violet eyes or the luxurious black waves of her hair, she would have commanded attention. The way she moved, the way she spoke, every action seemed deliberate and powerful. Sienna had watched her countless times on TV, analyzing haunted locations and communicating with spirits, but seeing her in person was unreal.

"Dylan," Ashlyn greeted him with a warm voice. The crystal pendant around her neck shimmered as it caught the ambient light, drawing Sienna's eyes.

As the two spoke, Sienna tried not to gawk. The paranormal had always fascinated her, and here she was, standing in front of a celebrity in that very field.

"And you must be Sienna." Ashlyn turned to her, a smile lighting up her face. Her gaze was intense, making Sienna feel both scrutinized and seen. As Ashlyn clasped her hand, a chill shot up Sienna's arm—an unexpected sensation.

Sienna swallowed her initial nervousness and smiled. "It's an honor to meet you. I've followed your work for years."

Ashlyn's laughter was light. "Thank you, dear. And while I haven't known of you for years, the spirits, it seems, have been eager for our paths to cross."

The admission sent a thrill through Sienna. She pulled out a chair and sat down, feeling the reassuring touch of Dylan's hand on her shoulder. The air in the room grew heavy as Sienna locked eyes with Ashlyn. The intense violet seemed to pierce right through her, as if reading her soul.

"I've felt her," Sienna whispered, her voice shaky. "Eliza. Following me, watching me."

Ashlyn fixed on Sienna with a penetrating gaze. "You, dear, have an undeniable connection with Eliza, something that goes beyond mere coincidence. Perhaps it's a shared emotion or experience that makes you particularly receptive to her energy. Spirits are drawn to those with whom they share deep resonances. It's as if your souls echo similar tunes."

Sienna blinked. "Are you saying that Eliza is… reaching out to me because she sees a part of herself in me?"

Ashlyn nodded. "Exactly. And this connection might make you sensitive to her presence and emotions. It could be why you've been feeling her so intensely."

Dylan cleared his throat, drawing their attention back to the apparition he'd encountered. "And the woman on the road? Was that Eliza's doing?"

Ashlyn's expression darkened. "Yes, that was indeed Eliza, but her intentions weren't benign. Her pain and anger have muddled her perceptions, making it hard for her to see past her rage. She might view you as a threat, or perhaps as someone akin to those who wronged her in the past."

Dylan swallowed hard. "So, she was trying to…?"

"Harm you," Ashlyn finished. "You need to be cautious, both of you. Eliza's emotions are tumultuous, and her actions are unpredictable."

Dylan's grip on his glass tightened, his knuckles whitening. "But why? Why now? Why through Sienna?"

Ashlyn continued, her voice soft but with a steel edge, "Because of your connection, and because of Sienna's. Eliza sees in Sienna both an ally and a weapon. She's using Sienna's ties to the past, her very blood, as a conduit to reach you. Manifestations, especially ones as powerful as this, thrive on unresolved emotions. It's what gives them strength, what binds them to the realm of the living."

Ashlyn leaned forward, her fingers playing with the rim of her teacup, her violet eyes sharp yet understanding. "You see, curses, in their truest essence, are about grief, anger, and vengeance. And when powerful emotions remain unsettled, they bind spirits to the realm of the living."

Dylan shifted, eyes flitting around the room before settling back on Ashlyn as she continued.

"Eliza is very much tethered to this world. Her anger, her sense of betrayal, it's what keeps her anchored. And John," her eyes flitted towards Sienna, "he's trapped in her shadow. His love for her is still profound, but he's hesitant, conflicted. He wants to reach out, but her overpowering rage keeps him at bay."

Sienna found her voice. "So, what does this mean for us, for Dylan and me? Is there a way to... I don't know, appease Eliza's spirit?"

"Eliza's anger is directed at the Whitmore lineage, and Dylan, you are in the line of fire." Ashlyn took a deep breath. "As for you, Sienna, being tied to the Goodwin line, she will see you as a tool, a means to inflict pain upon a Whitmore."

Dylan's fingers tightened around Sienna's, his face paling. "How do we stop it? There has to be a way."

Sienna added, "Is there a way to free both Eliza and John, to let them find peace?"

Ashlyn pursed her lips. "It's complex. To break a curse, especially one so deeply ingrained, one must first understand its origins, its true essence. It's not just about pacifying a spirit; it's about resolving the root of that intense emotion."

She paused, taking a sip of her tea. "There might be a way, but it will require delving deep into the past, confronting truths, and possibly facing dangers. Are you both prepared for that?"

Dylan's jaw set. "Whatever it takes. I can't—I won't let this curse continue to harm those I care about."

Sienna squeezed his hand. "We'll face it together."

"Then let the journey of unravelling begin. The spirits have spoken, and they are waiting." Ashlyn smiled. "To confront and find resolution, both of you need to face Eliza at the site of her heartbreak on the Frozen Tears Trail. The tether binding her spirit to this realm is strongest there. Together, you both must be present and unified."

Sienna's heart felt like a stone sinking into the chilling depths of a brook. Images of Eliza danced in her mind, accompanied by the haunting silhouette of John, her star-crossed lover. Sienna couldn't shake off the eerie sense of connection to Eliza, maybe because of their shared lineage or the echoing patterns of fate. The burden of history and intertwined destinies pressed on her.

Dylan squeezed her hand. "We'll face it together," he promised, then turned to Ashlyn. "What should we expect? And what about John?"

"Ah, John. He's bound by the same emotions but hidden, overshadowed by Eliza's raging spirit. If we reach out to Eliza, calm her turmoil and guide her towards understanding, then John will naturally gravitate towards her." Ashlyn tilted her head and smiled. "The hope is for them to find solace in each other and be united in peace."

"So, there's a chance they can be together in the end?" Sienna asked. "After all this time?"

Ashlyn nodded. "Indeed. Spirits, like living beings, seek resolution. And John has been waiting, silently, for his beloved. If all goes well tomorrow, they'll find each other."

Sienna took in a breath, her eyes watery. "Then we have to do it. Not just for us, but for them, too."

Ashlyn leaned forward, her voice dropping to a whisper. "Prepare your hearts. This journey you're embarking on is not just about ending a curse; it's about mending broken souls. Remember that."

As they made their way out of the pub and back to Sienna's car, the weight of the impending evening settled between them. The atmosphere in the car was thick, filled with a silent understanding of what was at stake.

Dylan broke the silence, his voice low and steady. "I've got some things to handle tomorrow during the day, but I'll pick you up in the evening. We'll drive together to The Frozen Tears Trail."

Sienna cast him a sidelong glance. "What about your car?" she asked.

He gave a sheepish grin. "I've got another one."

They drove back in silence. Once they reached Sienna's place, Dylan leaned over, placing a gentle kiss on her forehead. "Rest up. Tomorrow will be... intense."

Sienna nodded, watching him go, then made her way inside.

In the quiet of her room, with only the soft hum of the ceiling fan broke the silence, Sienna laid on her bed, moonlight casting gentle shadows across the walls.

The revelations of the day weighed on her. Her connection to Eliza, Dylan's family curse, the looming showdown—all wove together into a complex tapestry of history, destiny, and emotions. And her feelings for Dylan? They added yet another layer to the mix. Were they just replaying an ancient love story, or was it a new, dangerous entanglement in their own right?

She mulled over Eliza and John, the tragic lovers. The possibility that her and Dylan's fates might be linked with theirs was both haunting and oddly romantic. Could they change the course of their histories and carve out a future for themselves?

Meeting Ashlyn Alden added an exhilarating edge to everything. Sienna had been following Ashlyn's shows for years, and now to meet her in person? It was surreal. Ashlyn was a part of the puzzle in this intricate web of past and present, and Sienna was eager to see what insights she would bring.

CHAPTER EIGHT

Whispers of Deception

The gentle rhythm of rain against her window lulled Sienna into a reflective state. In the muted light of her room, she let her thoughts wander, the glow from a lavender-scented candle casting dancing shadows on her walls.

Eliza Goodwin. The name echoed in her mind. It felt so surreal, being connected to someone from a different era. Sienna wondered what Eliza had been like, how she dressed, the songs she liked, and the dreams she had for herself. It felt like they were kindred spirits in some bizarre way, and Sienna couldn't shake off the feeling that she needed to help Eliza find peace. Was this her new life now? Channeling spirits, decoding age-old mysteries?

And then there was Dylan. A rush of butterflies took flight in her stomach at the mere thought of him. This wasn't like her past flings or those college dates that ended in awkward goodbyes. With Dylan, everything felt amplified—the chemistry, the emotional roller-coaster, the intrigue. Plus, he was just... different, complex, and fascinating, even if his family history was a tad more than she'd bargained for.

The reverberation of a firm knock echoed through the room, wrenching Sienna from her reverie. When she opened the door, there stood Dylan's grandfather, his gaze piercing and familiar—it mirrored Dylan's own striking blue eyes. Eyes that had borne witness to decades of hardships, now fixed on her with a disconcerting intensity. His presence carried the weight of a lifetime's guardedness, a hardness forged by trials, that rendered her at once humbled and intimidated.

"Sienna," he announced, stepping past the threshold without waiting for her consent.

Her breath caught as the room seemed to close in with his entrance. "Mr. Whitmore," she responded, her voice a mask over her rising apprehension.

He surveyed her small quarters, his eyes pausing just a beat too long on the lone candle flickering by her bed—an unsettling reminder of her vulnerability. "My grandson holds you in high regard," he started, his voice a chilled timbre, seasoned with years of skepticism. "But does he truly see who you are?"

Tension coiled within her. "I've been nothing but honest with him."

A cynical smirk twisted his lips, devoid of warmth. "Is that so? Or are you merely spinning yarns to ensnare his heart? Because if so, it will end poorly for you."

Her heart thudded, taken aback by his blunt accusation. "I've done nothing to deserve that."

He stepped closer, his presence looming like a storm. "You tread dangerous ground, young lady. The Whitmore legacy is steeped in burdens and old blood—not tales for the faint-hearted." His expression softened, revealing a glimmer of the anguish beneath his stern exterior. "I once lost someone dear to me, a casualty of the very shadows you and Dylan flirt with. The ruin it leaves in its wake is profound."

There was sincerity in her voice when she spoke. "I'm truly sorry for your loss."

He dismissed her with a wave. "Spare me your pity. I need you to grasp the weight of your actions. The repercussions." He drew a deep breath and presented an envelope from his coat. "Consider this a lesson. Take it, leave

Dylan be, and spend your summer elsewhere. You'll receive your pay, regardless."

"And if I don't?"

His eyes, icy and unyielding, met hers. "Then you'll find yourself without a job. I'll see that you leave with nothing. As for Dylan? I'll inform him you sought to leverage our family for money. It will hurt him, but he'll move on, recognizing you for the opportunist you are."

Tears threatened her resolve, but she fought them back. "Why are you doing this?"

A shadow of deep sorrow flickered across his face before it was masked by resolution. "I've seen too many drawn to our family with false pretenses, seduced by our wealth. I've suffered enough heartbreak, and I refuse to let Dylan endure the same fate, not at the hands of someone like you. Loyalty to the Whitmores runs deep; betray that, and the fallout is severe."

Sienna straightened as she met his challenging stare. "I care about Dylan," she declared, her tone unwavering. "I'm not here for your money or your name. My feelings for him are genuine, and I will not betray him."

He studied her for a tense moment, his scrutiny heavy. "Perhaps you believe that now," he conceded, weariness seeping into his voice. "But life's winds shift swiftly. Today's certainties can evaporate by tomorrow."

He placed the envelope on a nearby table, a symbolic gesture laden with temptation. For Sienna, it wasn't just paper; it was an escape from debt, a gateway to a future free from financial worry.

Yet, as she considered it, her thoughts returned to the many nights spent with Dylan under the stars, dreaming of a different future together. She remembered his passion, his vision for a different path for his family's resort—a vision not bound by old money but by new ideals.

Her decision made, Sienna extended the envelope back to him. "I can't accept this," she stated, her voice steady despite the storm inside.

His eyebrows arched, surprise flickering across his features before his expression shuttered once again. "You're rejecting a secure future."

"I'm choosing a chance at something real," she countered, her chin lifted in defiance.

A tense silence fell, heavy with unspoken threats. William exhaled, a sound of reluctant respect or perhaps resignation. "Very well. You've made your choice," he said as he turned toward the door. Pausing, he added without a backward glance, "Remember this decision. Whatever comes next is on your head."

Sienna watched him leave, her heart racing. She felt a mix of fear and determination, but above all, clarity. Dylan

deserved to know the truth, and together, they would face the storm that was coming their way.

Her feet carried her to the parking lot, the gravel crunching beneath her boots. She had envisioned the evening to unite forces - herself, Dylan, and Ashlyn, coming together to lie to rest spirits that had roamed for too long. But when she arrived, the space where Dylan's car should be waiting greeted her, sending a pang of unease.

Her hand slipped into her bag, pulling out her phone. She scanned the messages, hoping for a late notification, an explanation. But none came. Her fingers began typing out a message to Dylan. *"Where are you? We're supposed to meet now."*

Seconds that felt like eons passed. The dimming sky, painted with strokes of twilight, seemed to grow darker with her mounting anxiety. The phone buzzed. A message from Dylan.

"I can't believe you'd try to extort money from my family. Was all of this just a play for my family's fortune?"

The message felt like a punch to her gut. Sienna's eyes blurred with tears. How could he think so low of her? After the moments they shared, the dreams they weaved, the connection they felt. She felt the weight of William Whitmore's manipulation, the depth of the trap she had walked into.

Desperation fueled her response, fingers trembling over the keys. *"Dylan, how could you believe that? After everything, after all our conversations, the time we spent... I'd never... How could you?"*

She sent the message, waiting for a reassuring reply, a call, something. But as minutes stretched on, and the cold, indifferent parking lot lights blinked to life around her, she felt the sting of isolation and betrayal. The silence of the evening was broken only by the distant murmurs of the resort, and inside, Sienna's heart wrestled with the painful twist of events.

With heavy steps and a heavier heart, Sienna trudged back to her quarters. The once comforting trees and paths of the resort now seemed oppressive, their looming shadows reflecting her turmoil. She needed the sanctuary of her room, a few moments to process the whirlwind of accusations and emotions.

But as she rounded the corner, the sight that met her was far from welcoming. Two burly figures in resort security uniforms stood outside her door, looking grim.

"Miss Avery," one of them, a tall man with a graying beard, addressed her with a mixture of pity and formality. "We've been instructed to inform you that your employment at Whitmore Resort has been terminated, effective immediately."

Sienna's heart raced. "What? On what grounds?"

The second officer, younger and more uncomfortable, shuffled his feet. "Orders from the top. You have 24 hours to vacate the premises."

Sienna's eyes widened in shock. The reality of her situation sank in, amplifying her sense of betrayal. "So I'm just being thrown out like some... criminal?"

The older officer sighed. "Miss Avery, we're just following orders. This comes from Mr. William Whitmore himself."

She felt her cheeks burning, tears threatening to spill. "Does he even know the reason?"

The younger guard shifted. "We're not privy to those details. We've just been told to carry out these instructions."

Sienna steadied herself. "Alright," she said, voice shaking but defiant. "Give me a few minutes to grab some things. I'll come back tomorrow for the rest."

The older officer nodded, a hint of sympathy in his eyes. "We'll wait out here. Stop by the security office when you are ready for the rest."

As Sienna stepped inside her room, anger and confusion engulfed her. With each item she threw into her bag, she replayed the events of the day, wondering how everything had unraveled. It wasn't just about the job or the accusations; it was the shattered trust, the hurt of being misunderstood and falsely accused.

She folded her clothes and stuffed them into her suitcase as memories of hushed conversations and sideways glances from other employees flooded back. They had whispered words of caution about getting too close to the Whitmores. She had brushed off such warnings as mere workplace gossip, perhaps even jealousy. But now, she saw those warnings in a different light.

William Whitmore's stern admonition echoed in her mind. *"Cross the Whitmores, especially when it comes to family, and you'll regret it."* She realized his words weren't just a threat; they were a promise.

Yet, amid the shadows cast by the Whitmores' power and influence, what wounded her heart most deeply was Dylan's silence.

Sienna zipped up her bag. She had to see Dylan and look into his eyes so he could see the pain and confusion that his family's actions had wrought. If, after that, he still sided with his family's unfounded accusations, she would know where she stood.

One thing was clear: Sienna would not leave without a fight. The Whitmores might have their legacy, their sprawling estate, and their deep-rooted power, but she had truth, grit, and determination on her side. And she was not one to be silenced.

Navigating the hallways of the resort wasn't a simple task for Sienna. With each step she took, unspoken judgments bore down on her. The sidelong glances, some full of pity and others laden with scorn, stung like a slap. While being the epicenter of a scandal was both unfamiliar and unsettling.

Suddenly, she spotted Maya, a friendly face among the throng of unfamiliar and judgmental ones.

"Sienna, wait!" Maya rushed towards her, concern in her eyes. "I heard... I mean, everyone's talking about..."

Sienna raised a hand to stop her. "I know what they're saying. But it's not true, Maya."

Maya nodded, her lips set in a tight line. "I believe you. But you know how it is here—the Whitmores are untouchable. Everyone just believes whatever they're told."

Sienna sighed, feeling the weight of the situation. "I thought I could change things, maybe even break the cycle."

The two women shared a moment of understanding. It was clear that the family's influence had long tentacles, touching everything and everyone associated with the resort.

"Be careful, Sienna. Not just with the family, but... with everything."

Sienna smiled. "I will."

Maya took Sienna's hands and squeezed them. "Whatever you decide to do, just know you've got friends here, okay?"

With a grateful nod, Sienna moved past the crowd and towards the exit, her head held high. She might have lost her job and the budding relationship she had with Dylan, but she was leaving with her integrity intact.

After the harrowing exchange with Maya, Sienna trudged to the parking lot and hurled her suitcase into the trunk of her car. Closing her eyes, she drew upon every shred of courage remaining within her. One last task lay ahead before she could contemplate her future moves.

Cool marble from the family wing corridor chilled Sienna's hastened steps. In her turmoil, the hushed ambiance of the space felt almost mocking. The grandeur of the Whitmore estate loomed intimidating and hostile.

As she approached the ornate double doors leading to the heart of the residential wing, her resolve intensified. But before her hand could even rise to knock, a stern-faced staff member stepped in her path.

"Miss Avery," he began, his tone rigid, "you're not permitted here."

Sienna's desperation was clear in her voice. "Please, I just need to see Dylan. I have to explain."

But the man was unyielding. "I'm sorry, but Mr. Whitmore has given strict instructions. The family is not to be disturbed tonight."

The weight of rejection and the reality of her isolation from Dylan's world pressed on her. She was on the outside, and those imposing doors were ensuring she stayed there.

Sienna squared her shoulders, her voice unwavering, "I'm not leaving until I see Dylan."

The employee shifted, his face showing traces of sympathy but bound by his role. "Miss Avery, I understand how you feel, but if you don't leave, I'll have to call the police."

Before Sienna could respond, the shrill ring of her phone sliced through the thick air of tension. Recognizing Ashlyn's name on the display, she answered.

"I am so sorry we are not there yet!"

The mystic's voice carried a note of concern. "Where are you both? I was expecting you two by now."

Sienna hesitated, then recounted the evening's events. She could hear Ashlyn's soft sigh on the other end.

"Oh, Sienna... this is a difficult situation."

Sienna felt her heart pounding. "I don't know what to do, Ashlyn. I need to see Dylan to clear things up. But I also understand the urgency of what we have planned."

There was a pause before Ashlyn responded. "Sometimes, we have to make choices that aren't easy. The spirits are important, but so is setting things right. You will make the right decision."

Sienna took a deep breath, her mind racing. "I'll come by myself. If I stay here and get arrested, it won't help anyone. And maybe, just maybe, once this curse is lifted, everything else will fall into place."

Ashlyn's voice was gentle. "Very well. I will see you soon."

Sienna, still smarting from the abruptness of her recent confrontations, was just about to succumb to a tearful retreat when a feeble but clear voice interrupted her.

"Miss Avery, is it?"

Pausing, Sienna looked up and saw a woman whose body bore the undeniable marks of chemotherapy but whose eyes sparkled with sharp intelligence. Mrs. Whitmore, Dylan's stepmother, looked Sienna over with a discerning glance.

"Mrs. Whitmore, rest," the employee admonished, stepping forward with a protective stance.

She waved him off, her voice keeping its clarity. "Rest? I've been resting all day. Had a little fall earlier." She gestured to a nearby room. "Come, Dylan is in my sitting room. He wouldn't leave my side, even when I assured him I was alright."

Sienna's heart swelled with relief and continued confusion. The pieces weren't aligning.

Mrs. Whitmore continued, "Dylan mentioned he had plans tonight, and he's been searching for his phone. I suspect he wanted to tell you he'd be running late. These things happen when you're watching over a clumsy woman." Her wry smile hinted at many stories untold.

Sienna blinked away the moisture in her eyes, words failing her. Mrs. Whitmore gestured towards the entrance to the family wing. "Come, let's get this sorted. There's no reason a misplaced phone should lead to so much drama."

Gratitude welled up inside Sienna as she followed, more hopeful about the evening's prospects and her relationship with Dylan.

The opulence of the Whitmore family wing was undeniable. Antique portraits of stoic ancestors adorned the walls, and plush carpets softened their steps. Mrs. Whitmore led Sienna to a comfortable sitting area, where a tray of tea sat ready, its steam curling up like fragile wraiths.

"You must wonder why my son stood you up," she began, her fingers wrapping around a porcelain teacup. "I had a minor fall today. Nothing serious, mind you, but enough to cause a fuss." She rolled her eyes, smiling. "Dylan... he has a heart as big as the ocean. He refused to leave my side until he was certain I was alright."

Sienna's heartstrings tightened. She'd known Dylan's warmth, his deep sense of care, but this...

Mrs. Whitmore continued, "I've been in your shoes, dear. Marrying into this family wasn't... smooth. William has always had his ways. He protects the family name, its reputation, often came before everything. Even happiness."

Sienna took a shaky breath, feeling the weight of William Whitmore's manipulations. "He offered me money to leave," she confessed, her voice a mere whisper.

Mrs. Whitmore sighed, nodding. "It's not the first time, and it likely won't be the last. But you, my dear, you've given Dylan something precious—hope, joy, a glimpse of a life beyond these gilded walls. I've seen the way he looks at you. The way you light up his world."

The door burst open, catching everyone off guard. Dylan stood there, looking disheveled with worry marking his features. Yet, when his gaze settled on Sienna, the worry transformed into surprise and relief.

"Sienna," he exhaled, bridging the distance between them to envelop her in a heartfelt embrace. In that single touch, amidst the surrounding chaos, their worlds seemed to find their balance again.

"I'm so sorry for not being at the lot. After the fall," he looked into her eyes, regret etching every line of his face. "I was so focused on Mom and then... I couldn't find my damn phone to call you."

Sienna touched his cheek, trying to calm the self-blame she saw there. "It's not just about the phone, Dylan. Your grandfather..."

Dylan's expression hardened, a storm brewing behind his eyes. "What did he do?"

She took a deep breath. "We'll talk, but for now, just know it's not your fault."

The floors echoed their footsteps as Mrs. Whitmore ushered them to the exit. Her eyes sparkled with mischief. "Now, you two better hurry," she murmured, the corners of her lips curling into a knowing smile. "This family has waited long enough for a change."

Outside, the evening had deepened into shades of dark purple and blue, with stars lighting up the sky. A cool breeze carried with it whispers of love, betrayal, and a curse that had lingered far too long.

Dylan looked down at Sienna, tightening his grip on her hand. "It's hard to believe all that's happened," he said, his voice filled with awe and a touch of regret. "But we're in this together, all the way to the end."

Sienna nodded, buoyed by his commitment. "Every twist and turn today has brought us here. It feels like the universe is steering us to correct a mistake."

The expanse of the estate lay before them, a land rich with memories of joy and pain. The surrounding trees seemed to be cheering them on, their leaves rustling in encouragement.

Approaching their destination, Sienna stopped and looked up at the vast night sky. "Despite everything, I have faith in us," she whispered, her voice steady with resolve. "Tonight, we'll alter the course of Whitmore history."

CHAPTER NINE

Frozen Tears

The luxury of Dylan's backup car unsettled Sienna. Knowing about Dylan's affluence was one thing; seeing it in such stark display was another. She couldn't help but ponder the extent of the Whitmore family's possessions.

Her fingers traced patterns on the plush leather seat. Although the overt wealth made her uncomfortable, thoughts of Dylan's stepmother brought relief. The woman's genuine warmth seemed out of place in a world brimming with privilege. Sienna found comfort in the notion that not all money corrupts, hoping she might eventually accept this facet of Dylan's life.

As the car wound along the road, Sienna tried to dismiss these thoughts, instead taking in the scenic beauty. Trees lined the road, their branches interlocking above like a secret handshake from the past. The world outside was draped in muted blues and silvers, the moon playing peek-a-boo through the leaves. Every splash of moonlight on the ground seemed to dance, lighting the path to The Frozen Tears Trail.

Sienna turned to Dylan. The dashboard's soft glow cast his features in gentle contrasts, highlighting a furrow of concern on his brow. Their eyes met, and their hands came together, fingers entwining, mirroring the trees above.

The winding road ahead seemed to stretch, both of them cocooned in their own thoughts. Dylan broke the silence. "What did my grandfather do?"

Sienna took a deep breath, turning to Dylan. "Your grandfather offered me money—a lot. He wanted me to leave and never come back. He even offered to cover my college expenses, just like that."

Dylan's grip on the wheel tightened. "What did you say to him?"

Her voice wavered as she replied, "I won't lie. The thought of being debt-free and starting fresh was tempting, even if just for a second. But then I thought about us, all our moments, everything we've been through. I couldn't walk away without telling you."

He exhaled. "I know it's been hard for you, Sienna. Grandfather can be persuasive, making offers that seem too good to turn down."

Looking away, she gathered herself before continuing. "After I refused, he changed. He threatened to make it look like I was after the family fortune." A tear escaped down her cheek. "And when I tried to message you, the replies... they didn't sound like you."

Dylan glanced at her. "I saw him watching you earlier and felt uneasy, but I didn't imagine he'd go to such lengths."

Sienna intertwined her fingers with his. "It's clear he wields a lot of influence, even over you, to some extent. Family dynamics are complicated."

He met her gaze, his expression conflicted. "I should've seen through his tactics. I should've been there for you."

She leaned back. "It's uncanny, isn't it? How our situation mirrors Eliza and John's. It feels like we're caught in a repeating pattern."

Dylan nodded. "It does, but this is now. We don't have to repeat the past. We can make our own way."

She smiled. "Exactly. We have what they didn't: hindsight. We can use that to our advantage."

"You're right," Dylan squeezed her hand. "They didn't get to fight for their love. We do. We can make our own ending."

A comfortable silence fell over them, punctuated only by the hum of the engine and the whisper of the trees outside. Both were acutely aware of the challenges ahead—not just with appeasing restless spirits, but in carving their own path into a world strewn with obstacles.

Dylan glanced over. "I hate to see you hurt by my family's schemes. Let me help. I could use my influence to get your job back. It's the least I can do."

Sienna turned to him. "This isn't about the job. It's about principle. I value your support, but I'm not a damsel in distress you can rescue with money. I've always stood on my own two feet and I don't want that to change now, even if we are together."

He parted his lips to argue, but she cut him off. "This isn't about pride. It's about my identity, my self-respect. I refuse to let your grandfather's actions define me."

Dylan sighed. "I get it. I just wish I could do more."

Her smile softened. "Being here, understanding and supporting me—that's enough. I'll figure the rest out."

As they neared the trailhead, the surrounding air seemed to grow heavier. "Your stepmother... she's truly remarkable, isn't she? Like a ray of sunshine."

Dylan nodded, his smile genuine. "She's always been a guiding light through the chaos of my family."

After parking, they retrieved flashlights from the glove compartment and faced a narrow dirt trail concealed by overgrown foliage. There was only one other car in the lot, likely Ashlyn's. Sienna shivered, admiring that woman's bravery for venturing into the dark to appease the spirits. Then she remembered her own nighttime hike.

Stepping onto the trail, they began their trek through the woods, illuminated by the moon's pale glow. The rustling leaves and the distant calls of an owl composed a natural symphony around them. With each step, the atmosphere thickened, charged with what was to come.

Sienna felt the damp, cold ground beneath her, her senses sharpening in the night's embrace. Thoughts of Eliza played in her mind, imagining what she might have felt on her fateful walk through this same place.

The soft murmur of water grew clearer, guiding them onward. After navigating a slight incline and maneuvering around twisted roots that seemed to emerge from the earth's very core, they reached the clearing that cradled the small brook where they had first found the post.

Under the moonlight, the water shimmered, casting playful reflections on the surrounding trees. The serene yet melancholic sound of the flowing water wrapped around them.

Emerging from the shadows near the brook was Ashlyn, her flowing robes merging with the essence of the night. Their meeting at this charged location was intentional; tonight marked a turning point in the long, intertwined histories of the living and the dead.

The clearing felt different now—not just a picturesque spot beside a brook, but an arena where the boundaries between the seen and the unseen were thin. Three figures stood at the water's edge, their shadows stretching out long and wavering. The torches Ashlyn had placed in a protective circle around them casting a warm, orange hue. The flames wavered and danced as if touched by an unseen force, their movements mirroring the chaotic whirlwind of emotions enveloping the trio.

Ashlyn, her posture erect and commanding, motioned for Sienna and Dylan to join hands with her. Their fingers intertwined, the shared warmth a contrast to the cool night air. Ashlyn chanted, her voice resonating, the words unfamiliar yet evocative. Each syllable seemed to pull at the very fabric of the world, reaching out to those who existed just beyond the veil.

The brook seemed to respond to her call, the gentle murmur of the water growing louder, as if the spirits of the water itself were listening. Sienna's heart raced, feeling the energy of the place seeping into her, grounding her and heightening her senses. Every sound became acute.

Dylan's grip tightened around Sienna's hand. She could feel his apprehension, but there was also a determination, a resolve to see this through. Their shared experiences, culminating in this very moment, made their bond feel unbreakable.

Minutes felt like hours as Ashlyn continued her incantations. The temperature dropped. A cold mist rolled in, blanketing the surroundings and sending shivers down their spines. The still waters of the brook began to roil and churn, icy tendrils snaking out onto the bank.

Out of the freezing mist, a spectral form took shape. Eliza materialized, her visage clear against the warm glow of the torch flames. Her ghostly attire, reminiscent of her time, was encrusted with frost. Her eyes bore anger and resentment from the decades of torment.

Just outside the silvery glow of the clearing, John's spectral form stood alone, a sorrowful guardian watching over the scene. He tried to communicate, but Eliza, consumed by anger, couldn't perceive him.

Spotting the ghost, Sienna gasped in surprise, her eyes widening. "John's here!" she whispered, pointing toward the spectral figure. Realizing he had been observing them all this time added an extra layer of complexity to their mission.

"Why have you summoned me?" Eliza's voice was laced with bitterness.

"We're here to help," Ashlyn replied, "to end the suffering that's bound you to this place."

Eliza's icy stare fixed on Sienna and Dylan. "More Whitmores? The very root of my pain?"

Sienna stepped closer. "We've seen the toll of this curse. We're here to offer peace."

Eliza's laughter hung in the air. "Peace? After all that I suffered? Each Whitmore generation pays for what they did to us."

"We know your pain," Dylan intervened. "We're familiar with your love story with John, and want to set things right."

John's spectral form strained, his mouth opening, trying to speak, but no sound emerged.

Eliza's tone was filled with heartbreak. "Every night, I yearn for him. But we remain separated, our souls forever reaching but never touching."

Sienna replied, "John's still here. Please see him and let us help you break this tragic loop."

Doubt danced in Eliza's eyes. "But John's moved on, hasn't he? My only solace has been vengeance against the Whitmores."

John tried to move closer, his eyes desperate, begging her to recognize his presence.

"It has to end. For both the living and the departed," Dylan pleaded. "Sienna and I, we feel your pain. We're living it."

"John and you, you had love," Sienna added. "Help us. Let us help you find the peace you deserve."

Eliza seemed conflicted, her form flickering. "Seeing you both, willing to risk so much for love... Reminds me of what John and I had."

Ashlyn intervened. "John's love was genuine. It's time you both find peace."

"Please. Let's end this torment." Sienna approached the ghost.

Eliza hesitated. "I want to believe there's hope."

A gust of wind rustled through the trees, carrying faint, haunting whispers with it—echoes of old accusations and betrayals. The voices fed Eliza's doubts, stirring memories of past deceits.

Suddenly, the air turned icy cold. Eliza's anger flared again, her form growing darker. "Whitmores, always deceiving! How can I trust any of you?" she hissed.

Before Dylan could respond, an icy grip clutched his throat, lifting him off the ground. Panic surged as he struggled for air.

Sienna screamed, "Eliza, no! Please!"

Consumed by fury, Eliza seemed beyond reach. Dylan's face turned a dangerous shade of blue. Beside her, John's form brightened, his mouth moving in a silent, desperate plea. Despite his efforts, the chains of Eliza's wrath rendered him invisible to her. His expression was one of deep anguish as he witnessed the unfolding scene.

Ashlyn, summoning all her strength, chanted a potent incantation, attempting to counter the overwhelming energy Eliza radiated. The torch flames flickered wildly, casting eerie shadows that moved in sync with the escalating clash between the living and the dead.

John's gestures became more frantic, his pleading eyes filled with urgency.

The atmosphere around the brook darkened as Eliza's wrath intensified, her focus narrowing on Dylan. Her eyes, burning with a supernatural glow, fixed on him as she declared, "The blood of the Whitmores! They're the root of my suffering!"

A chilling wind enveloped Dylan, draining his warmth and turning his skin a ghastly pale. As frost crept up his neck and face, Sienna watched in horror, realizing he was close to succumbing to the same fate that had befallen Eliza. His eyes showed his torment as his breaths grew shallower and more infrequent.

Then a cry cut through the clearing. It wasn't from any of the living, but from John, his spirit stirred by the cruel replay of his own past. With desperation and love, he broke the silence, calling out, "Eliza... please."

The fierce spirit halted, her focus momentarily shattered. From the deeper shadows by the brook, John's spirit emerged, his face full of pain and regret. "It wasn't the boy. It was me. Don't blame him for my actions."

Eliza's gaze flicked between John and Dylan. "John?" her voice wavered. "Why did you leave me? I trusted you with everything!"

John's spectral form approached her. "I was weak. Promises tempted me. By the time I realized the consequence of my choices, it was too late. But please, don't continue this cycle of pain and revenge."

Dylan, weakened by the attack, murmured, "I'm... I'm so sorry for what my ancestor did. But please, let us help you find peace."

"This cycle of pain and revenge won't bring you happiness." Sienna approached a shivering Dylan, clutching him close to her, and added, "Let us help you both find each other, find love once again, and rest."

Eliza's spirit looked torn, her gaze shifting between Sienna, Dylan, and John, who reached out a translucent hand towards her. "Come to me. Let us find peace together."

But Eliza cried out, "He's gone! He left me to freeze, to die alone and heartbroken!"

"I never left you, my dearest." John's voice, filled with raw emotion, echoed through the night. "I've been here, tormented by my decisions, wishing I could change the past. Let's not let another generation bear our pain."

Eliza looked at John as she released Dylan, tears of frost forming in her eyes. "Is it really you?"

John nodded, reaching out to her.

Sienna watched with relief as color crept back into Dylan's cheeks. His breathing grew steadier, the frost retreating from his skin. He coughed and opened his eyes, meeting Sienna's concerned gaze. She pulled him close, feeling the returning warmth of his body and the strong beat of his heart against her chest.

Around them, the brook's waters calmed, the restless ambiance giving way to deep silence, broken only by the gentle crackle of the torches. The world held its breath in anticipation.

Eliza hesitated for a moment. The years of betrayal and sorrow still lingered. John reached out to touch her ethereal cheek. "My love. I am so sorry. I should have been there for you."

She responded, her voice trembling, "You left me. Alone in the cold, betrayed by love."

John nodded, his spectral eyes filled with tears. "I know, and that guilt has tormented me every moment since. I wish I could turn back time, do things differently. But now, we have a chance, here, together."

The two spirits moved closer to each other, their forms intertwining, hands reaching out to hold one another. Eliza rested her head on Jim's shoulder, her anger melting away in the warmth of their reconnection.

Sienna whispered to Dylan, "They deserve this moment, after all they've been through."

Dylan nodded and squeezed her hand. "It's time for healing."

Ashlyn's eyes sparkled under the torchlight as she started another chant, her voice blending themes of reconciliation, forgiveness, and new beginnings. The surrounding energy shifted, becoming lighter.

As her chant reached its peak, John and Eliza, now fainter, shared a tender, lingering kiss—a symbol of everlasting love that transcended life and death.

The brook, reflecting their reunion, shimmered under the moonlight, mirroring the two spirits as they dissolved into countless motes of light that rose and danced in the night sky.

Overwhelmed by the beauty of the moment, Sienna felt tears well up. She turned to Ashlyn, her eyes questioning. "Is it over? Has the curse truly been lifted?"

Ashlyn surveyed the now peaceful surroundings and took a deep breath, soaking in the renewed energies. "Yes," she said. "Their spirits have found peace and are finally at rest."

Dylan turned to Sienna. "It feels like a weight's been lifted, doesn't it? Like we've been holding our breath, and now..." He inhaled deeply and exhaled.

Sienna nodded. "Maybe, just maybe, we can start to move forward."

Dylan looked into her eyes. "Their story has ended, but ours is just beginning."

Ashlyn's eyes shimmered with wisdom as she smiled at Sienna and Dylan. "The spirits are reunited," she said. "Being part of your journey has been a privilege beyond words. Remember, the essence of love is to bridge souls and mend what was once broken." She glanced around and her words echoed through the clearing as if meant for more than just those present.

Her robes rustled as she gathered her belongings and moved towards the forest's edge. Bathed in the silver light, she paused and looked back. "Cherish these moments and let this sacred ground strengthen the bond you're building."

With an effortless grace, Ashlyn disappeared into the depths of the forest, leaving Sienna and Dylan alone in the clearing.

As the past's remnants dissipated, Sienna felt a surge of sensations. The ambient energy of the clearing, tinged with the centuries-old feelings of Eliza and John, enveloped her. She almost believed she could hear Eliza's voice, echoing the ache of long separations.

Dylan caught her gaze with a deep, understanding look. He reached out and touched her cheek. "You feel it too, don't you?"

Their faces drew closer, and their lips met in a kiss. It was gentle yet profound, bridging centuries of longing with the freshness of new affection.

As they parted, Sienna breathed deeply, feeling overwhelmed by the intensity of the moment. "It's like we're not just us. We're them too—Eliza and John, somehow," she whispered.

Dylan nodded. "It's powerful, isn't it? To feel so connected to the past, yet right here, right now, it's just you and me."

The cool night air seemed to echo their realization. A gentle breeze rustled the leaves, and the moonlight cast a soft glow that enveloped them.

"Look at the brook," Sienna said, pointing towards the gently flowing water that shimmered under the moonlight. "Even it seems calmer, like it knows."

Dylan squeezed her hand, his smile tender. "Maybe it does. And maybe we can find our own peace, too."

"Tonight feels like a new beginning," Sienna said, her voice filled with hope.

Dylan agreed, his eyes bright. "A new beginning for us, free from the past but enriched by it. Let's see where this journey takes us."

Hand in hand, they turned away from the brook, each step forging a new path in their story, under the vast, starlit sky.

CHAPTER TEN

Rooted in Love

In the dim glow of the motel's aging lights, Sienna climbed into the bed she once shared with Dylan. The room was charged with echoes of their past intimacy, casting a patchwork of shadows and muted reflections. Outside, the chirp of crickets blended with the steady hum of the air conditioner, a lullaby both eerie and comforting.

As sleep tugged at her eyelids, Sienna's mind drifted—to the brook, to Eliza and John, and inevitably, to Dylan. The weight of the past few days pressed on her, as if the spirits of old lingered, whispering their stories and sorrows.

But tonight, as Sienna sank into sleep, an unexpected figure appeared in her dreams. It was Eliza, no longer a vengeful ghost, but a vision of timeless beauty. Her gown, flowing and iridescent, shimmered like dawn's first light. Her eyes sparkled with calm wisdom, transcending time itself.

"Sienna." Eliza's voice was a gentle whisper, like a breeze through autumn leaves. "I've come to thank you."

Caught in the dream's surreal embrace, Sienna responded, curiosity coloring her tone. "Why now, when you can finally be with John?"

Eliza drifted closer, her presence soothing. "Because of you, I'm free from centuries of torment. You bridged what seemed impossible. Now, before I become a mere echo of a forgotten tale, I want to share some wisdom."

A flicker of uncertainty crossed Sienna's face. "What do you want to tell me?"

Eliza locked eyes with Sienna. "Love fiercely, against all reason. Cherish it, for it is the purest magic. Don't let past mistakes bind you. Walk forward with Dylan. Let your light together outshine our dark past."

Tears welled in Sienna's eyes, her fears surfacing. "But how can I be sure it's real? How do we avoid heartbreak?"

Eliza touched Sienna's cheek as lightly as a snowflake. "You can never be certain, Sienna. But that's the beauty of love—it's a leap of faith, a commitment of courage. Follow your heart's rhythm; it will guide you, as mine did, on a perilous journey. Let love be your compass, even when the path is clouded."

A profound peace enveloped Sienna, comforting her as dawn's light began to seep through the curtains. Her connection with Eliza, forged through shared trials, would remain a part of her forever.

As she awoke to the new day, Sienna's heart felt lighter, blessed by Eliza's spirit and filled with a new resolve. With every heartbeat, she felt an irresistible draw to Dylan. Their intertwined destinies, once shadowed by history, were now ready to forge a new future.

She stretched, the cool sheets whispering against her skin. It was a truth she could no longer deny, a new dream in her heart. True, she wanted to travel unknown terrains, to pen down tales from ancient towns and bustling metropolis. Sienna aspired to be a travel writer, a blogger who'd capture the very essence of places and people. Yet, amid this yearning, was another—she craved to have Dylan beside her, as both her muse and confidant.

Sienna stretched under the cool sheets, a new dream blossoming in her heart. She envisioned herself traversing unknown terrains, capturing the soul of ancient towns and vibrant cities through her writing. The notebook on her bedside table, filled with blank pages, seemed to beckon her, ready to absorb tales of adventure and romance.

In her mind's eye, she traveled through bustling markets, serene mountaintops, and down cobblestone streets of charming villages. Dylan was there in each scene, his insights adding depth to every experience.

Compelled to share these dreams, Sienna grabbed her phone to message Dylan. She poured her heart and ambitions into the text.

Just as she hesitated over the 'send' button, a knock at the door caused her to pause. The insistent sound pulled her back to reality, and with a flutter of anticipation, she opened the door. Dylan stood there, his eyes brimming with hope.

"I know we agreed on a day apart, but I couldn't wait," Dylan admitted, his voice shaking. He seemed to search for the right words, his gaze flitting away, then back to hers.

Moved by his presence, Sienna reached out, her hand touching his cheek, and then pulled him into a gentle kiss. It was a kiss that spoke of reunions and resolutions, sealing their understanding in a moment of quiet intensity.

Dylan's initial surprise melted, his arms eventually coming around to hold her close. When they finally parted, their bond felt renewed, more solid than ever.

"Let's start the day together," Sienna suggested, stepping aside to let him in. They moved to the small table by the window, where the morning light cast a hopeful glow.

Together, they planned out a day of simple joys—visiting the local bookshop, walking through the nearby park, discussing her travel ideas and how he could be part of that journey.

As they talked, the notebook lay open between them, its pages filling with notes and sketches, plans for future adventures that they would document together. Dylan's laughter and enthusiasm enriched every plan, making Sienna's dreams feel even more possible. Whatever challenges they might face with others, like Dylan's family, they were ready to face them together.

"Let's make it official and introduce you to my family," Dylan proposed later, his tone light. Sienna smiled, a touch of nervous excitement in her expression. She agreed, knowing that facing his family was the next step.

As they arrived at the family wing of the resort, Sienna's heart raced a touch faster. As the great doors opened, a wave of warmth enveloped her from Dylan's stepmother. The gentle crinkle around her eyes and her inviting smile hinted at an unspoken understanding.

As the aroma of a lavish feast filled the dining room, Sienna couldn't help but feel a twinge of discomfort. The wooden table at the center was laden with an extravagant spread, mirroring a grand festivity that seemed at odds with her simpler tastes. Conversation flowed around her, shifting from light anecdotes to deeper discussions about the future.

Dylan's grandfather showed a surprising change. His demeanor had softened, the hard lines around his eyes replaced by a semblance of peace. Still, the grandeur of the setting was hard for Sienna to reconcile with the man she remembered—one who had openly doubted her intentions because of her modest background.

Dylan's grandfather was a man of formidable presence and strict traditional values and had not changed overnight. His acceptance of Sienna was reluctant, shaped more by resignation than genuine approval. After dinner, he summoned Sienna with a nod, his voice carrying a rare tremor as he addressed her.

"Miss Avery," he began formally, his tone lacking its usual harshness but still far from warm. "I've lived a life deeply rooted in our family's legacy, a legacy I see now that Dylan is ready to redefine. The strength of your commit ment... it is undeniable."

He paused, his eyes searching Sienna's. "Our past is a stubborn beast, yet the future—your future with Dylan—is yours to shape. I see that now. And while old habits die hard, your place here... it is acknowledged."

Sienna felt a surge of emotion, her eyes brimming with tears at the unexpected affirmation, however grudging it might be. It wasn't the warm embrace she might have hoped for, but it was a step—a nod to her potential role in Dylan's life.

As they rejoined the group, Sienna sensed a subtle shift in the atmosphere. The oppressive cloud that had loomed over the Whitmores seemed lighter. Dylan's grandfather's stern gaze met hers again, and this time, there was a glint of something that might pass for respect. Dylan and his father bridged the gap with small talk that, for the first time, didn't feel entirely forced.

Dylan, brimming with energy, began sharing his ambitious plans for the resort. "We owe it to this place," he began, "to not only preserve its heritage but also its environment. Eco-tourism and sustainability are the way forward."

Sienna watched as Dylan's father and grandfather leaned in, intrigued. "Eco-tourism?" His father raised an eyebrow. "What sort of changes are you envisioning?"

Before Dylan could answer, his stepmother jumped in, her eyes sparkling with pride. "He's been researching and making plans for months now. You'd be amazed at what he's come up with."

Dylan shot her a glance. "It's about balance. Making the resort a place of sustainable luxury while ensuring it doesn't harm the very beauty it showcases."

His grandfather drummed his fingers, contemplating. "And the business implications?"

Dylan's eyes gleamed. "Imagine guests coming to White Pines, not just for the luxury, but for a unique experience. We'll integrate the natural beauty of the surroundings into every facet of their stay."

His father quirked an eyebrow, intrigued. "Go on."

"We can have guided eco-tours, showcasing the native flora and fauna, and perhaps collaborate with local environmentalists to educate our guests." With enthusiasm in his voice, Dylan described this place as a hub for both relaxation and personal development.

His stepmother nodded. "The land here is full of potential. It's a brilliant way to make use of it."

Dylan's grandfather steepled his fingers, his eyes assessing. "And the accommodations?"

Dylan grinned, "Eco-friendly cabins. Solar-powered, built with sustainable materials. Minimizing our carbon footprint while offering a unique, luxurious experience. The spa can use organic, locally sourced products. The restaurants can shift towards farm-to-table dining."

His father looked thoughtful. "And what about the long-term profitability?"

Dylan responded, "By branding White Pines as an eco-luxury resort, we'd be targeting a niche but rapidly growing market. Time is about more than just profit, but legacy. We'll be setting a standard, drawing discerning guests who will pay a premium for ethical, sustainable luxury."

Sienna squeezed Dylan's hand under the table. She loved how his vision wasn't just about revenue, but about making a lasting positive impact on the environment and the community.

As Dylan finished, there was an appreciative hum around the table. His stepmother beamed with pride, but it was his father who broke the silence, turning his gaze to Sienna. "And what about you, Sienna? Apart from working at the resort, what are your other pursuits??"

Sienna hesitated for a moment, the attention on her. "Well, I've been working my way through college. I've always had a love for words and stories, so I'm majoring in literature."

Dylan's stepmother smiled. "Ah, a storyteller. That's wonderful."

Sienna's face lit up, her initial hesitation fading. "Yes, and my dream is to combine that with my love for travel. I aspire to be a travel writer, capturing the essence of places and cultures, the hidden stories waiting to be told."

Dylan's father stroked his chin, eyes narrowing. "That's an interesting combination. Travel and literature. With

White Pines moving toward an eco-luxury brand, having authentic stories and experiences documented could be beneficial. And considering the Whitmore Group has resorts and hotels around the world…"

Dylan caught on. "Sienna could document her experiences, offering an authentic perspective on each location. It would be fantastic branding, connecting with audiences on a personal level."

His grandfather, not one to be easily impressed, nodded. "It's not a bad idea. People resonate with stories, with genuine experiences. It could set our brand apart."

Dylan's stepmother added, "And it's always wonderful to support young talent, especially when it aligns with our vision."

Sienna hesitated, processing the sudden turn of events. She was wary of wealth and its trappings, and being thrust into the Whitmore family's world was both overwhelming and a tad suspicious. However, the prospect of earning her place, on her own terms, was enticing. "I appreciate the sentiment," she began, "but I would like to finish college before making any major decisions. Education has always been important to me."

Dylan's father raised his hands in a placating gesture, his eyes twinkling with mischief. It was clear where Dylan got that grin. "We're just speculating right now, young lady."

He winked at her. "The door is always open. Take your time."

After their heartwarming conversation at lunch, Dylan took Sienna by the hand, leading her toward a gardener. With a brief exchange and a knowing smile, the gardener handed Dylan a small sapling.

As they approached his car, Sienna's eyes were filled with questions. "Where are we going?" she asked.

Dylan just smiled, a glint of mischief in his eyes. "You'll see."

They drove in companionable silence, the world outside shifting from the manicured beauty of the Whitmore estate to the wilder, untamed landscapes. They arrived at The Frozen Tears trailhead.

"This place," Dylan started, "will always be ours. It's intertwined with pain and tragedy, but I want us to change its narrative. I want this place to be a symbol of beauty, joy, and our love."

They walked to the brook, a young sapling cradled between them. Together, they planted it at the water's edge.

"This tree," Dylan said, holding the sapling, "will grow alongside our love. Strong, enduring, always reaching for the sun."

Sienna brushed her fingers over the young leaves and smiled. "Every time we come here, we'll see its growth."

Together, they stepped back to admire their handiwork. Under the canopy of trees, with the gentle babble of the brook in the background, they envisioned a future brimming with hope, love, and growth. The haunting legacy of Eliza's curse was now reborn as a living testament to enduring love.

About the Author

Beth Connor is a weaver of tales, captivated by writing and fueled by a love for storytelling.

Beth's creative pursuits are a reflection of her life philosophy, and she is always searching for new ways to expand her knowledge and understanding of the world. She has a keen eye for detail and a remarkable ability to create vivid, dynamic settings that resonate with her audience.

Beth's talent has earned her recognition as the author of several published works, including the captivating novels "Hollow City" and The Isdralan Chronicles Series as well as a contributor to many anthologies. Beth is also an accomplished audiobook narrator and the host of the popular podcast, "Crossroads Cantina."

Despite her many endeavors, Beth remains down-to-earth and dedicated to living authentically, true to her passions and values. She resides in the Pacific Northwest with her husband, two children, and canine companions, who bring her boundless inspiration and delight.

Also by

ALSO BY BETH CONNOR:

Hollow City

<u>The Isdralan Chronicles:</u>
Micah and the Candles of Time
Prodigy of Flame
Bridge of Blood and Thornes

<u>Kindred Spirit Mysteries:</u>
The Secret of Misthaven Island
Bridging the Heart